Joe P.

no Joe, no b

Simple as that.

Thanx!

Ed

OUR WAR
and How We Won It

Every life is many days, day after day. We walk through ourselves, meeting robbers, ghosts, giants, old men, young men, wives, widows, brothers-in-love. But always meeting ourselves.

JAMES JOYCE, Ulysses

Contents

OUR WAR
and How We Won It

I Break into Houses

There it is. This is what I do, straight out and up front. I used to work New Rochelle north of Beechmont Drive but the coloreds moved in with all kinds of relatives and a Doberman pinscher. All the money is tied up in General Motors. They get a few bucks, do they buy silverware or Van Gogh? No, they go down to Dick Gidron and trade in the Buick for a Sedan De Ville. Like I said, I'm not a car thief; I break into houses.

Right now I work the Lawrence Park section of Yonkers. Lawrence Park West. Bronxville P.O.s. The big Tudors where you can walk around upstairs for three-quarters of an hour even when everybody's home.

Three weeks ago I toss a nice eighteen-, twenty-room Greek Revival on a wooded acre. St. Charles kitchen, half-dozen fireplaces, professionally decorated, etcetera. You get an eye for these things after a while. Sometimes you look at the drapes for the color combinations and you want to puke but this place, like I said, is very, very well done. Real Persia on the carpets. Heavy as a bastard these rugs so you don't even look twice except for the aesthetics of the thing. You start to appreciate. This is if you have the time, if everybody is away or something. You case a house, you watch the people, you get to know what's what, who's who, etcetera. I don't have to tell you everything, right? Your place I could probably get into with a credit card or even a good shoulder on the kitchen door. But what would I get? A couple of twenty-five-dollar savings bonds and a pewter mug if I'm lucky. Some stainless-steel forks? An old tweed Botany 500 overcoat with holes in the pockets? Don't say no because I've been down that road. I probably started in a neighborhood just like yours when I was a kid.

That's how a kid gets started in this business, with a place like yours. Who else would break into a broken-down joint that needs paint where the guy can't even afford to fix the potholes in the driveway? What do I get from a place like yours except agida? And you feed a hundred-and-twenty-pound German shepherd two cans a day and watch him shit on your Woolworth's rug his whole life because you're worried I might come in and steal your calendar Timex and that crummy half-filled bottle of eight-year-old Scotch you probably have stashed someplace in the kitchen. I say to you now: forget it. I do you one favor. I tell you to relax. There is nothing in there that will do me any good. Anyone who breaks into a house like yours is a dangerous character. Give him what he wants. He is probably crazy enough to hurt somebody.

How did I start doing this is now what you want to ask me. It started the year I was in Catholic school when we moved here from down South. My daddy was an army man, a captain, commissioned, with a thin moustache, close-set eyes and a mean streak that wouldn't quit. He never had to beat me much, he just grit his teeth a lot and squeezed them pig eyes at me and I knew close where I stood. He would holler like a crazy man, which he was, because later he ended up in St. Alban's with snot running down from his nose that he wouldn't wipe off. They even shaved his moustache for him and he didn't do nothing about it. That's how layback crazy he became. And this from the guy who dreamed of commanding armies. He thought he was George Patton or Teddy Roosevelt or somebody and all the time he's got only one oar in the water. When they recruited him, somebody must have seen them pig eyes and said this man will be a good soldier, we will need him for the next war.

Meanwhile me and little Ralphie Zurk are breaking into houses. Wednesday they had religious instructions and the nuns would let all the Catholic kids out early so the other Catholic kids from the public schools could come in and learn catechism. So here go me and Zurk into the first house. Zurk is this skinny kid, nervous, irritable and fighting all the time after school. Stone, looking-for-trouble personality. Looking back I wonder how I got hooked up with somebody like Zurk in the first place. I mean me, an officer's kid. His old man was an E-4, a broken-down amateur boxer who taught Ralphie to do the dukes and he was pretty good.

Maybe we're eleven years old when we go into the first house, a tiny Cape down off Woodland Avenue with hardly no yard at all, but there is this big wild hedge growing maybe ten feet tall that stretches one whole side of the property and creates what people in my business refer to as a blind, meaning an area where you can get in and out without somebody watching you from the bathroom window next door.

Zurk tapes a little section of the window on a side entrance, wraps his knuckles in a handkerchief, raps the glass, and it cracks easy, all without a sound. He peels the tape with the broken glass away, reaches in and unlocks the door and here we go. What we were looking for was gold watches and diamonds and, of course, cash. I look back now and what would you do at that age with a ten-carat diamond ring besides wear it or give it to Mary Ann who sits next to you in English. We figured a fence was what you put around a playground. Needless to say, there was no diamond ring in this place. This place is what a crook today would call an Archie Bunker house and there's nobody in the world would break in here except a couple dopey kids like us or some drunk Archie Bunker neighbor who mistakes the house for his own and thinks his wife locked him out again. But Pete Rose wasn't born in Cooperstown. You start someplace no matter what you do for a living.

So what we got from this palace was double-0-zero. The guy had three or four pair of khaki pants hanging on hooks in the closet and a bunch of lumberjack shirts and a green uniform that had a patch over the tit that said something like "Eddie" or "Tony" in script. The bastard didn't even own a sport coat or a second pair of shoes. His wife's closet, on the other hand, was full of all kinds of shit, spangled dresses and cocktail hats and I remember one of those wraparound-the-neck things with an animal's head still on it with phony bead eyes but the fur was even worn off in some places like it was handed down to her from some old bag in the family who was probably hot shit in her day.

Neither one of them has any change in the bureaus so we went through the khaki drawers hanging in the closet and came up with emptiness, so we threw all her shoes in the toilet and we dumped the khakis and her crap and the dead animal fur in the tub, put in the stopper and started the water running. Downstairs, we broke all the plates in the kitchen and pulled the plug on the refrigerator so the milk goes bad and everything else in there would rot. You don't have to tell me this doesn't make any sense because I know that. I'm not eleven years old anymore. What can I tell you? Besides, people still do this kind of thing, people fifty years old, out of spite. They make comments to try to ruin somebody's cocktails. It's the satisfaction thing, just like pulling the plug on the ice-box. The victim only feels a little bad, plugs the thing back in and goes on with his life, but there's a class of squirrels who feel better doing this like they're in charge of somebody's action for a minute or two. Over the past few years, my business has given me the leisure time to study the psychology of these things.

Anyhow, we carved our initials into the dining room table before we left and this is how I got caught for my first burglary. This and the fact that somebody saw Zurk's blue-and-white Shelby with the rusted wire basket leaving the house. Zurk held out for a few minutes and then he told them everything, like how it was all *my* idea and how I threw the shit in the tub while he just watched and kept telling me I shouldn't be doing all of this, that it wasn't the right thing to do. Then he tells them that *I* had told him about these other houses I had broken into and he gives them addresses and dates and everything and it turns out that old Zurk was a housebreaker from way back. The cops don't fall for this and they figure it's the both of us all the time. Case closed. I'm released in my old man's custody (all this happens before he completely wigs out), he has to pay the damages and I take one of the true classic beatings of all time. And don't tell me about the Firpo-Dempsey fight. I'm talking about a 220-lb. sadist army officer with two pig's eyes six months away from a strait-jacket doing a tap dance on a little kid's head. This was some serious shit.

So then I started getting more stiff about my life. I tried to study. I tried out for the basketball team, etcetera, but it's no use. I'm branded bad news and the parents tell the kids to stay away from me and Zurk. They are headed for the prisons. They are rotten eggs. What becomes of Zurk I don't know because the next year Pops does the looney tunes and I get switched to this army junior high school at Fort Slocum where they march you around from morning to night and try to make you a little soldier. But even back then, a day doesn't go by that I don't learn something. Here are the names of some bombs: atom, shrapnel, guided missile, hydrogen. These are things that they drop on you. Let's say you're a Jap or a Russian, then one day some pig-eyed kid out of Long Island University who studied airplanes down at Pensacola flies over you in an F-4 or an F-15 or a B-35 or something and ruins your whole frieken day.

And some of the other things they shoot your way are: bullets, disease pellets, nerve gas capsules, mortar, and hand grenades. A direct hit by any one of these things will ruin your plans for the weekend. I wouldn't be a soldier if they made me a colonel and threw a party.

So what I did then was to start breaking into houses around the base. Not for nothing, just to get a look at what was what. Didn't even snatch nothing the first few places, just looked around, chowed down and split. And I started my antiwar campaign. Right now I'm very, very upset about these people who are trying to start up the draft. They would like to put kids in a bunch of uniforms and send them to the Persian Gulf. I sense a mood around these days that says let's go burn these guys, rip off their 450SLs, whip the camel-shit-eating bastards back into the deserts they came out of.

I say steal the lames blind before they know what's what. Move the pyramids at night over to San Diego where the American public can enjoy them. They have helicopters now that can do it. They don't tell you that. They save this stuff for the heavy dancing. They've got invisible planes with black pilots you don't see at night. All Americans. Educated right over here in the Northeast. You don't even know their names. They have no names. Their teeth have been pulled and they can see through closed eyelids by a drug. This is the kind of stuff they don't tell you. They don't want you to get alarmed. In certain ways, they are very thoughtful. And I know, by the way, that the pyramids are in Egypt. Please don't try to second guess me that way. You knew I was talking about the oil and you said to yourself how does he get Egypt into this thing. You are poor because you are rude. And if you do happen to have a few bucks, your children will blow it because you teach them only how to drive.

Now: One day early on in my career, I see this thing that reminds me of the Maltese Falcon. It's on a bookshelf in this prep school guy's house on the base who's a captain out of Brown University ROTC. A man of consid~ taste with the name of Wentworth. Maybe two in the army and he goes back to the s~ winter evening where he came from man's bank. But the marble bird he n~

is my first serious artifact. Today it watches from a pedestal everybody who passes down the hall of my personal home and it is the topic of conversation beaucoup. And this is saying something because the competition is fierce. I have some things that should be in the Metropolitan Museum of Art. Two small pieces in fact once were.

There is something about the first bird to a serious-minded burglar that is nothing short of exquisite. To a thief of accomplishment, there is always that one special thing early in his career that turns him from expensive junk to an appreciation for the simple and the lovely work of a true artisan. It is like the first farewell from a thirty-year-old bottle of Scotch whiskey to a fat Irishman. From that hour forward, the J&B bottles he will break on the hood of his car.

Lastly, I must tell you that I have very few friends in my line of work. One, people like to rat on you to porky to get themselves out of a jam. And two, I have a different, liberal type of attitudes from the run-of-the-mill burglar. I voted Kennedy in '60 and Humpty Dumpty in '68. By nature, felons and etcetera are very conservative politically, not that they vote so much, but they feel that we should take no shit from China or Russia or no one like that. It's a macho thing. You should be so lucky to have *me* break into your house compared to these guys. Whatever is hanging, I don't touch nothing by Dali and I won't fuck around with prints, signed or otherwise. Cash I will take but no credit cards or blank checks. I am not a Puerto Rican from a truck or a Polish immigrant.

So, where have I been between the time my old man's eggs scrambled and now? It's so easy for a kid to end up like this, you say, a kid from a broken home with a pop who butters his hand instead of his toast. What happened in all the middle years? Can you picture the squalor? The packs of chain-smoked, butt-end rooms? The shitcans next to the mattress, the night-time neon pulsing through the curtainless, paint-peel windows, the godless, drunken homosexuality, the lack of love, the world according to wimp, the Chicken Delight with a paper shot glass dripping with rancid cole slaw, the three thousand bottles of Night Train wrapped in brown paper bags, the toothaches, the heartbreak of psoriasis?

Man, you are some gullible piece of work. You'll believe anything. You crave the incredible like white craves rice. You are some ponderous bag of shit. You think because you work for Con Ed or Arnold's Bakery that you're better than a house burglar? You think it's more noble to steal a hundred bucks for sitting inside a manhole all day listening to the Yankee game than what I do? Or forging cookie and bread chits in the A&P and Gristede's?

Let's first clear up the facts. What happened to me was, I bought Micronetics at 4. Beehive at 2, Burger Palace at sixty cents. These are stocks, George, look 'em up. Read 'em and weep. And I don't use Wall Street Discount either. Merrill-Lynch, One Liberty Plaza. I am now (may I say this without offending?) one heavy-packing son of a bitch. Ready Assets, by the way, I forgot to mention. And porkbelly futures. Chrysler I'm still looking. I watched Lee Iwannnacocacola on TV at the hearings where he was asking for two billion. I give him ten cents and a ticket back to Hoboken. I confuse him with the other guy, the one who runs the Yankees. Two fog horns. Flub and Tub. Two Bogarts without baggage. Can you see these two bazookas together in Hickey-Freeman suits going through each other's pockets like in an old fast-speed movie? Still, they got money. The only way somebody dopey like you makes a killing in the market, you shoot your broker.

If I am by one chance mistaken, and you are a person of substance, all I'm looking for is maybe a nice Remington bronze and two real old Tiffany lamps in very fine condition, otherwise I'm golden. I will pay cash. Or maybe I'll see you at the house.

How Some People Feel About Jesus

I was working for the church, trying to help out at one of their bazaar things. They gave me a table. They said: Stand there and see what you can get for this stuff. Everything is marked, but you can go down. The less we have left at the end, the less we have to throw out.

They gave me the toy table, probably because I was new. They didn't want to give me the jewelry or the arts and crafts because they were afraid I would screw it up, so they gave me the toys—a lot of broken crap—plastic horses with three legs, metal cars with no wheels—you've seen this shit. And a lot of bent-up and ripped boxes of games—Concentration, Go to the Head of the Class, checkers, Careers, Clue. A lot of puzzles, a Mister Potato Head, a bunch of dolls, each with something missing—a shoe, an eye, clothes, an arm.

What it was, was a sad-sack table. I think what they

said was: Let him start with this stuff, see what he can do. If he can do it, next year we move him up to used clothes—that's if he shows up. Our church has a problem with people showing up.

I wore my blue blazer and chino slacks like I was going to spend a day on Ted Kennedy's yacht, thinking maybe when they see this, they'll give me the old furniture or the books where I could maybe meet an intelligent person. But no. They pointed to the junk table and said stand there and see what you can get.

Our church is loaded with these old broads who figure they're on their way to heaven. When the minister talks, they sit there in their little hats like potted plants with tiny smiles on their faces like them and Jesus got it all figured out. They still believe in the harps and the wings, like it's all going to be a big tea party with no smoking, where you flutter from cloud to cloud with a cup and a saucer in your hand. Sounds like a bunch of genuine sweethearts, right? Wrong. Cash this: When any one of them gets in charge of something, she ties one end of a rope to your feet and the other end to a saddle with a horse attached and she whacks the thing on his merry way dragging your face through the dust. I wear a blazer with golden buttons and they put me in charge of the junk. Am I missing something?

The first thing I get is some kids eight or nine years old who want to start screwing around with the only good thing I got, a big, plastic boat, an ocean liner with maybe six little lifeboats attached, swinging by tiny, thin chains. I tell them, take it easy with that, it's the only good thing I got. One of them tries to pull out a Little Orphan Annie game from the middle of a pile on top of which is the ocean liner and, crash, there goes the boat, the only good thing I got. Slides off the back of the table, wham, onto the floor.

"Get out of here" I tell them. "You wrecked the whole set-up here."

"I was trying to see the game" says the one who did it, a heavy-set, freckled, red-looking kid, the kind of a kid who grows up to drive a meat truck, the kind of a kid who grows up to have a mean-looking face sticking out at you from the windshield.

"It was an accident" says the kid, backing up.

"Your ass is an accident" I tell him.

As I'm picking up the cracked ship, trying to hook back a couple of the lifeboats, a voice comes over my shoulder. "Don't scream at the children" it says.

When I get up, cradling my ship, I see the woman, the babe from used clothing, the table behind mine, standing right there at *my* table looking like she thinks she's the angel who appeared to Mary.

"I didn't scream at anybody" I tell her. "Look what they did to this ocean liner. They cracked the shit out of it."

"And you used vulgarity to those children" she says. "This may be a meeting room, but we're still in God's house."

"What vulgarity?"

"You said *ass*."

"Well wa dee da" I said.

"Are you a member of this congregation?" she asks.

"Who do you think is passing the basket up and down the aisles on the left, Efrem Zimbalist Junior? I don't remember you. *You're* the one not in church much."

Fact is she looked so much like the other hags I wouldn't know if I saw her before or not. Just then we were interrupted by a man who shoved two quarters at me and had himself a grip on a couple of board games.

"Hold it up, Mack" I said. "Let's see those boxes so I can check the price."

"A quarter each" he says.

"Let's have a look."

He surrenders the boxes but all the time he's got this sour look on his face. "Go back to your table" I tell the old broad from clothing.

"The reason I'm here" I tell the gentleman in front of me, "is to check the prices and make sure the money's right. If everybody was honest, they could just have a bunch of unattended tables where you could help yourself and make your own change."

"May I go now, or would you like to check my identification?" says the wise guy as he shoves the two boxes under his arm and heads for the exit sign.

"You're unhappy because you didn't get a chance to cheat the church," I holler at him across the room so everybody can hear. And there he goes, storming out the door into the sun with his tail between his legs like the monkey he is.

So far, maybe an hour and a half into the gig, I got fifty cents and a broken boat which might tell you how some people feel these days about Jesus.

About then, here comes, from the back entrance, through the kitchen, like Friar Tuck, the minister. He is a roly-poly, squat-down little man who some years ago gave up a faltering career as an A&P manager to go into the ministry. He enjoys talking publicly and privately about the money his vocation has cost him. "The meat department alone" he says, "did ten thousand a day. Back *then!*"

"How are we doing, ladies?" he bleats, in his best impersonation of one of the robed Plantagenets. He has a habit, left over from when he was in charge of wrapping London broils in cellophane, of wiping the blood from his hands onto his gown. "Are we making money?" he laughs. Either the laugh of a man who sees something funny in the fools who are making change of quarters for Jesus or in serious respect for the value of American coinage.

He wrings his hands on his cloak and around and around he goes. He will disappear quickly, I have been assured. Channel Two is doing the Cardinals-Giants. But he will make his presence felt lest anyone forget who it is that makes it all possible.

"And how are we?" he asks as he approaches the junk table, the table with the broken boat, the table of the man with the blue blazer who rides herd on the junk.

"We is fine" I tell him. He has forgotten my name. "And how is your holiness?"

"Good, good. I'm glad everything is going well. What a *team!*" He does a little Loretta Young two-step thing by the kitchen entrance, faces the room, smiles broadly, raises both arms, then fades into the dim fluorescence of the kitchen which leads to the back door.

"Don't confuse the *man* with the *mission*" I say loudly to all in attendance, meaning it just like it sounded.

"Pipe down" yells an elderly lady at jewelry. Jewelry is an important table where all the super-crones nest, so I let it pass by and I try to shill a weighty, middle-aged woman who is standing at the end of my table carrying an old CUOMO FOR GOVERNOR shopping bag. She is eyeing some puzzles.

"Aren't they lovely?" I ask her. "I'll make you a deal on all of them, six for five dollars."

"They're marked fifty cents each" she says.

"Three dollars for all of them. What do you want from

me? We're trying to raise money for the missions."

There's a very unusual puzzle, a depiction of the Last Supper. The box cover is nice, sort of a stained-glass effect. "You picked out the most beautiful item on the whole table" I tell her.

"I don't think all the pieces are here" she says after opening the box.

"They're all there" I tell her.

"They can't be" she says. "It says on the box five hundred pieces. There can't be more than three or four hundred here at the most."

"No" I tell her. "It would be marked on the box if anything were missing. Nobody would turn in a puzzle with pieces missing."

"I'm telling you they're *missing*" she says. "Have you ever done a puzzle?"

"Of course I've done a puzzle" I lied. "I've done dozens of puzzles. Possibly hundreds. And I've never had one yet where all the pieces weren't there."

"Well this one is missing pieces."

"I'll make you a deal on it."

"I wouldn't mind" she says, "if a couple of apostles were missing, say on one end of the table. But you don't know. It might be something important. I wouldn't want to spend all that time and then find out, for instance, that Jesus wasn't there."

"He's there" I said.

"How can you be so sure when you obviously know nothing about it?" She looks at me accusingly.

"I can't be sure" I said. "But I'm pretty sure."

"How much is that ocean liner?" she asks.

"It's cracked" I tell her. "Two nitwit kids came in here and knocked it over. It's got a big crack down the side. It was the best thing I had and now it's got a big crack in it."

"I'll take it if you mark it down."

"It's only *two* dollars. Two lousy bucks. It's probably worth *five*, even with the crack. You can put it in the tub, pretend it's the *Lusitania*, watch it go down with everyone aboard."

"I'll give you a dollar."

"What about the puzzle?"

"I don't want the puzzle. I like to know what I'm getting."

I gave her the boat for a buck and I told her to get away from me and go chisel somebody else.

That night I put the puzzle under my coat and took it home with me. I opened up a bottle of Night Train and worked on it up to the point where I had Jesus right there in the middle where I knew he was. Just to prove a goddamned point.

One-Eyed Jacks

They were playing Rummy at the kitchen table. They were drinking gin with tonic, picking up and discarding playing cards. Andy was the bartender at the place Bob and Mary Alice used to hang out while they were married. Now Andy and Mary Alice had a thing going. Bob lived in Stamford in an apartment. Andy lived in Bob's house sometimes but mostly at his own place up the line in Norwalk or someplace like that.

After the separation, Andy asked Bob did he mind. Bob said no, he didn't mind. He had nothing to say about it. It was over and you can't keep minding forever, he said. That was life. Bob figured if it wasn't Andy, it would be somebody else. At least Andy had a job, sort of. Not that it meant anything since Bob still paid all the bills, but it was nice that Andy had a job, someplace to go instead of just watching TV. He couldn't call him a bum, really. He was just pretty much a bum. Bob didn't want to see Mary Alice with a bum. If she were living with a bum it would have made the memory of his marriage seem small, like Mary Alice could do bums or businessmen, it didn't matter. He didn't want the added burden of having to think that he just stumbled into the courtship and marriage by chance.

Bob had two Jacks and two Two's. His drink was empty and he wondered whose job it was to fill it up. He figured he was sort of the guest even though he knew where the bottles were kept, how to crack the ice trays, where the cocktail napkins were stored in the drawer under the sink. Andy was the host. Why didn't he fill up the goddamned gin?

"How's business?" Andy asked as he threw down another Jack. Bob bounced his empty glass a little, reaching too quickly for the Jack.

"O.K.," said Bob. Bob was an accountant for a Big Eight firm. He used to have a BMW, a blue one with leather, air, you name it. Now he had a Ford with a cracked window on the right side and a dent in the left quarter that was not big enough to meet the deductible. He used to park the BMW right in front of the bar where Andy worked. He and Mary Alice used to like it a lot. "I like the seat," Mary Alice would say about the passenger side. "The way you can make it go in any direction."

Andy picked up a card, but Bob forgot what it was that he had thrown down, what Andy needed.

"I don't think I could do that," said Andy. "Every day like that, just look at a bunch of numbers."

"It's what you make it," said Bob. He picked up another Two and felt like he was closing in on something. He wanted to beat these people.

"How about a refill?" asked Andy.

"Good," said Bob.

"Mary Alice?" said Andy.

"That would be nice," said Mary Alice.

Andy got up, stuck his fingers in the three glasses and headed on over to the sink. "Don't anybody look at my cards," he said. "I don't trust you people." He laughed in a sort of pre-drunk falsetto. Bob smiled as Andy looked at them from across the kitchen. Mary Alice laughed.

Bob looked down to his fanned-out hand. Three Two's sort of sat there like numbers, but the Jacks, dressed up in red and black, seemed like they were looking over their shoulders at him. Disdain was what it was, it seemed like. It was an old game with them.

Andy came back with the drinks for Bob and Mary Alice like he used to do at the bar, then he went back and got his own.

What's Left

When old Mom McArdle died that one night, January maybe, all kinds of shabby shit that had been stored up for years rattled all on its glass self selves, its ceramic pig bowl tops, its chicken salt pepper rooster vessel set beings and plates clicking china up side one another in the cupboard saying (and it *is* said), saying: Woooow! Get me out of this raggity-ass nineteen-o-four garbage can wallfront.

Worthless shit and they know it each. But worthless is one thing, knowing it is one more, and having to *exist* is a third, and worthless as you be, it still feel nice to have a little freedom, move (or *be* moved) around and see something new after fifty, sixty, seventy year of hanging out on one dead wall.

Worse for the shit, old plates, egg holder ducks, cheap glass glasses from the Esso station stacked up back inside the cabinets with wood doors painted up twelve times where you steady look out at the world is dark, man, dark and crowded up like a ride in a tool box subway.

It was Lu-Mae who first got the key and set her nose in motion through that place to see what it was she would like to have first before the rest of them got there for to divide up the loot. Lu-Mae is at one point seventy-two and rolling in her own count, wife to the son McArdle, Abner, a man who never got the ignition turned over on the vehicle of his own life and Lu-Mae would right like to get quick what's rightfully hers for to stuff up her own cabinet areas and get ahold of a thing or two or three that Slow Abner failed to provide as a *real* man should do all along for the woman he chooses out to sing in the movie of the music of his life like Nelson Eddy.

But no. Lazy Abner with a mind like a wall sconce set about in a plastic beach chair eating up corn on the cob or a sparerib for forty-eight years in the foyer of the trailer turning knobs on the Zenith try to get in a clear station. Now was her chance to get a little bit ahead in terms of worldly possessions. Don't be the fool who bets down against a woman owns a mission and a key to the door!

So Lu be dragging down old Heinz boxes from the attic area and filling up in it one by one jelly jars with the fluted bottom part, lemonade sets with the dripping down lemon pictures, Aunt Jemima canister set with the cover is the big black lady's head, a thick, pink vase and it would look good in the trailer breezeway with a solitary rose hanging out the top for the ladies of the trailer camp to see set up there when they drop by to shoot the shit. Each one very delicate item and artifact she wrap it up with the *Courier-Journal* sections just to see that it make the trip intact, no damage done. And the little glasses, spoons, hard-boiled egg cradles, ashtray say NIAGARA FALLS, VACATION PARA-

DISE, all of it go down to the box and say: Wooooow! Take us down on a ride from this nasty darkshit place. We ready now. But this old bitch be near to as old as the other old bitch. We be riding plenty more soon. Hallefuckingluya!

Iris, Edith, Clara are the other ones. Edith and Clara born of the blood McArdle. Iris married in, as luck would have it. And who the hell is Iris and Lu-Mae, out-laws, to think that they could pick an artifact from old Mom Mc-Ardle's treasure-trove of glassware and culinary serving trays? How can they do anything if they are ladies truly, but keep their goddamned mouths *shut*? Buttinski sons of bitches is what Edith thinks. And Clara. Don't make me say my curse, says Clara. Don't make me lose my fucking temper—I'll claw some of their eyes out and I'm the very one to do it too, if they get me mad. Are you listening to me Edith? We have to stick together on this one.

I'd just loooove to have that old shawl someday you're gone, Lu-Mae once to Mom McArdle and Clara right there, doing the dishes of all things whilst Lu sets her big dead can next to Mom Mac who was knitting on some wool skeins. And that old Seth Thomas clock for to remember you by each time it strikes up twelve. Wouldn't that be nice?

When Clara drove by the old brown run-down Mom McArdle house (she was on the way to the exercise class), she frowned to see what might be Lu-Mae's Dodge Colt parked in front wrong way to the curb with the hatchback in the up position. It had snowed, it had snowed so it was a tight squeeze getting down the road. Footmarks be all mashed in on the way up the walk, up the center of the old widewood stairs what lead to the porch. Clara's heart had a hurry-up. Her face all hot and her legs tensed up and her neck way out from behind the steering wheel like a male goose its testosterone has been right away hearing the bugle call. *That bitch is in my mother's house,* she screamed aloud. *She's got my momma's keychain.*

Wow. That's right, wow! Do you know these people? Here go Clara from the class of '34 barrelassing through the snowbanks, fighting her way up the porch stairs whoa— slipping up on a slick patch and down on all fours riding up them rails like the Hound of the Baskervilles. Foam and shit be running out from her mouth. I think she will *kill* this bitch.

Inside, she stop. Well hello, Mae. What in the world are *you* doing here?

Oh, say Lu-Mae, just *in*ventorying a few pieces. Getting everything ready.

Ready for what?

Oh, ready so everybody could pick out the things they want. So everybody can have a little piece of Momma McArdle.

I'm about to have a little piece of your narrow ass, you . . .

I beg your pardon.

What's in those boxes wrapped up in the *Courier-Journal*?

What boxes is that?

That fucking box right there next to your two size twelves. *That* one for starters.

I *don't* believe I care to hear that language. There are things here that Momma expressed while alive to me that she wished me to have in a personal way.

Where did you get the keychain to my momma's front door, bitch?

From Abner, of course. Abner would visit here in the dark days of Momma's illness which is more than *some others* bothered to do. Momma give to him the key to let himself in and out. I, of course, accompanied him every on and off. Blessed are those who visit for theirs is the Visitation.

Now, say Clara, I will once say to you, so you will not go about and tell the story that you were attacked from behind like a Jap or that you were caught unawares, that I will now *visit* you with claws and knees to the pubic area and strangleholds that you never even imagined that you did see on the wrestling shows. Put up your tiny, thieving paws and prepare to defend your scrawny-ass self as best you can.

I don't believe I'm quite hearing this.

Clara stepped all up on the boxes between them, crashing, crunching delicate artifacts. Lu-Mae's head was thrown back by Clara's forearm thrust, rather professionally dealt considering all the horrors of age that was on her. The women fell to the linoleum kicking and biting at body parts. Lu-Mae hadn't been involved in a physical altercation in sixty-five years, since that one time at the playgrounds, which is a long lay-off. Clara, on the other hand, had only recently done four good rounds with her husband, Walter. She fought him once or twice a year, regular season, go-for-it stuff, and Lu-Mae would have to jump up in class a whole lot to do Walter. Lu-Mae went all limp under her sister-in-law and Clara hadn't even yet raised a sweat. Knock old Lu-Mae's gray head into the linoleum a couple more times. Clara be up, now in the air, sweet Momma McArdle grease-hanging kitchen air, and her legs be extended out and come down strong on Lu-Mae's stomach with a butt-drop.

And this is what happens to bad girls, say Clara, raising

herself up from her knees. Somebody should of told you this when you was little. I've been doing exercise class for twenty-eight years, enduring all the little pains and agonies knowing that some day I would put an ass-kicking on you, sweetheart. I have smiled to you over the top of a teacup since nineteen and thirty-seven all the time thinking how some day I would bend your nosebone up to your eyelids. And God has given me that day. Dammit to *hell*! Now I can die and go to sleep.

I said Momma wanted me to have this stuff, scream Lu-Mae from her lost position on the floor. Her spine be propped up against the sink cabinet now. Her breath come puff puff.

Clara kick her way through the boxes of crap and reaching the main glassware cabinet, begin to smash figurines and bowls, tureens and candy dishes, throw them up against the far wall over the sink where Lu-Mae prop propped. Shards and chips of a lifetime of Momma McArdle's pack-rat philosophy come tumbling like starchips around her. Set there for what seem like months and years and she think finally to herself, to know precisely as she set with two eyes opened wide, wider than they'd ever been, what it meant, after all was said and done, to be an in-law, one who marries in. Momma McArdle hadn't meant her to have *anything*. Lu-Mae had about right deluded herself into this way of thinking. There was nothing for her here. Momma had given to her lazy Abner and that was enough.

And Clara be keep throwing dishes until the cabinets be emptied. Set down on an old wooden kitchen table chair and cross her arms like Dick Butkus stare directly down at Lu-Mae. Clara big bloated calfs be stuck out from under her cheap flower dress down to where they tied on to her thick-soled exercise shoes. Her face: Mean. Her eyes:

Scrunched-up. The sides of her mouth: All turned down like a sad old-lady dummy.

And this is the way always it end with an in-law. And if you don't yet know that, you soon will. Or later. Go ahead. Live.

The Second Law of Thermodynamics

Each day our universe becomes more and more disordered. Before our eyes and indeed behind them, distant galaxies recede at many thousands of miles per second. All of nature dictates a gradual but inexorable descent into chaos. This being the age of the penultimate skeptic, I ask you not to take my word. I ask you to look it up. And look around. For everything is coming apart and even as we contemplate this, the energy expended in the contemplation is irretrievable.

The man is in a train somewhere, a train laboring green and wooded hills of a foreign land. The private compartment in which he rides, although small, is decorated elaborately—mahogany walls, polished hardwood floor with a Persian carpet, a porcelain sink in the corner with thin gold handles and a long, narrow golden spigot. A beautiful bookcase, seemingly carved into one wall, holds dozens of leather-spined volumes. Three windows cased in the same highly polished mahogany and bordered by heavy, deep-crimson drapes afford a view which is at once soothing and eerie. He discerns that the inordinate beauty of the landscape strikes the visual sense with a charm unaffected more because of the absence of some things than the presence of others. It is untouched, unconstructed and simple nature. He wonders if it is the mind of an effete which equates beauty with the absence of humanity in any sense except in that as observer. Or are there two kinds of beauty? Or none?

He is a father and a husband in another land. He has thoughts of his children but these are unspoken, undelivered, perhaps invalid and worthless. A is to B as C is to D. And A is bad to B. It is an equation for a school child. He hopes his children are not yet up to equations, that still may be found time.

The body of foolishness drags like a sack behind him, pleasures both carnal and sweet. There is a taste left on the tongue which reminds him of what came before, of what he could have been with a different turn of the sun. He is a white man in his early middle years and he is on the descendant. It is the age of the black man and the age of the woman. It is time for the emerging nations and their peoples to repeat all the mistakes of history on their own. It is probably incumbent on them to do so. Speaking for himself, he never had a chance.

He passes a beach at Nice and all the women are topless. He is reading a Harlequin Romance and he senses that there is nothing for him to be ashamed of. He is beginning to get the feel of what elements go into making up a life. It is the order of insertion that remains mind-boggling. He thinks that perhaps all secrets sleep somewhere within the mathematics of a turning page. The

29

numbers are all there, like the bare-breasted women on the beach. It is the act of putting them together in the right order that defies imagination. All is experiment, and one life is much too quickly lived.

He has finished his book and is again in the train, in the fabulous room, a place he can't afford to be. He is a father and a husband in another land and he has no idea what it was that he didn't learn that has made his life evolve so poorly. Is man meant to be so alone, so introspective? Is each man, after all is said and done, simply an egocentric sun around which a primitive world revolves?

He thinks about his children reading books in another land, reading about Columbus discovering America. Their reading will get heavier. Soon. He despairs of time, the time left, time to tell them something, not something which will make him suddenly a true father in their eyes, he can't hope for that, but something that will give them the option of escape, a ladder from the fire. He wonders why he, as a father, especially as a father who has so little of value to give, feels obligated to pass anything to his children. He decides that it is in the nature of fatherhood. The least gift a father can bring is some bad advice based on a faulty understanding. A paltry package, but a gift nonetheless. Something. He hopes that they will know it for what it is—worthlessness born of the need to give.

He is framed in the window of a slowing train and he is elaborately made up, combed and dressed in what can only be described as the most flattering clothing. He wears a Picard watch, the center of which is an onyx-and-gold island surrounded by a sea of diamonds. He stands very still. He might be a mannequin. He senses that he may have been here, in this window for thirty-some-odd years and soon, as things slow, someone will come and mark him down because so few have shown interest. Around him are the most desirable and interesting items of tedium, each one of a kind.

Then he glimpses them approaching. They are politely shouldering their way through a crowd. His wife. His children. Those to whom he might have been a father and a husband. He wonders if they will pick him out—again, if they can afford it. It is to him a horrible, empty feeling to be part of such an absurd display. He wonders if they will recognize something in his eyes, in the rigid, stoical pose of his flat, pointless figure, something that will make them take him home. And he questions, if they do, when he gets there, can he change?

What Uncle Tom Did

My great, heavy father, while alive, used to wander from room to room about the house singing ballads, morose and ebullient from the Clancy Brothers' album. He had a voice, said my small, fragile mother, much like a horn from a dense fog. He sang of Brennan on the Moor and The Wild Colonial Boy. He sang all the songs of injustice and desperation and survival against odds insuperable.

He worked in those days for a wax company that was based in Massachusetts, and since we lived in New York he didn't have to work every day unless the mood was such that he couldn't help himself.

If the morning were bleak and dreary with that certain sorrowful pall that only the Northeast can show you, we would find him with our mother at the kitchen table with his large mitt wrapped around a coffee mug and she in her nightgown, sipping black tea from one of the small, fragile white-bone-china cups that Grandma had given her when they were first married.

"I suppose I'll go out and face the furies," he would say, tight-lipped, his little joke, but one so small and so often used that no one any more laughed or paid attention. "Waxes of the world, unite," he would say as if gearing himself up for the small adventures he would that day face: the unpolished asphalt tiles, the bare, dry, lifeless wooden floors of the lower East Side. On these mornings, he was groomed and elegant, at least as I remember it. Always a white shirt, a colorful tie, his hair parted neatly in the middle and giving off a wonderful, fatherly sheen and aroma of Old Spice and brilliantine.

But if it were a bright, clear, breezy morning and we were off from school on some holiday or summer recess, he would, just as the sun came yawning into the little room that my sister Coleen and I shared, barge in with his long, baggy drawers hanging down almost to his knees and pull us from our cots. He would carry us, one in each arm around the place, from room to room, singing songs that I now know to have been from *Oklahoma* and *Carousel* and *South Pacific*. It wasn't until later when the sun had for some time been up and things had settled down to a more thoughtful and serious routine that he would begin the Irish tunes. The songs always seemed to be about heroes, simple men usually, who, in the face of some great adversity, and filled with a love and compassion for their fellow man, and quick to sense the indignity in being shot at or imprisoned for no good reason, would strike out with a noble, selfless act at a morass of insensitivity, intimidation and bureaucracy.

"Trouble," my mother would say to us privately, "is what a person finds who doesn't keep busy at something. The more your time is filled up with activities, the less thinking you do about your problems." That she was talking about our father as well as trying to instruct us in the ways of a happy, uneventful life was something I didn't until years later understand. It wasn't until I was myself a grown woman, yoked with painful and uneasy commitments and fired by the need to see justice done, that I knew she was wrong. Not wrong in what she meant to say so much, but wrong in her definition of trouble.

As a child, I suppose you go through the days, one after another, expecting trouble. Is it wrong to think, as a child being constantly corrected, being read to from primers that stress brotherhood and decency, that it is not so easy as all that? Even early on you realize that you have to go about pushing and nosing into corners and demanding what it is that you need with the little language at your command. Trouble comes with life and trouble is concomitant with love.

There must have been a time when the differences between Mother and Father were much, much smaller than they finally became. It never really dawned upon me, and it couldn't have on Coleen who is two years younger, why it was that people got married in the first place. There were plenty of people to keep you company, if that's what you wanted. And most grown-ups didn't enjoy having kids around much, and those who did, it seemed to me at the time, could borrow them for a while from relatives if they needed to. There were plenty of kids around that no one big bothered with much. Even at family gatherings, we would all be sent off to eat in a separate room at a large, long, naked table with only one or two knives among us for the mustard and, later, the jam.

In the other room, there was cloth on the table, nuts in

a big bowl, cotton napkins, piles of silverware, foods of all colors and descriptions and many more glasses than they could possibly need. At our table, someone was always short a glass, and as many times as you were told to use your napkin, you were never believed when you said that you had never got one to begin with. And when you made an ugly face after tasting something terrible that they had put on your plate, they would tell you that one day God would freeze your face in that expression and no one would want you again. "It's frozen now," they would say. "Go up and look at yourself in the mirror." If it were one of the younger ones they spoke to, that one would push away from the table in terror, and head to the bathroom, which was always upstairs, in order to stand on the closed toilet and peer into the only mirror in the house accessible to the little people who ate at the long, naked table. No, children weren't the reason they married, of that there could be little doubt. We figured then that it was men who loved to eat and women who loved to do the cooking. It was the only thing that made any sense.

The trouble began, as do all great troubles, a child sooner or later learns, with a relative. Our trouble was Uncle Tom, my mother's younger brother. I remember him as a great walrus of a man, almost as large as my father, and with a fine, red, bushy beard that sank when he sat, down onto his chest and lay above an enormous belly, covered always by a plaid shirt that gathered outside his trousers over his second, lower, slightly less enormous belly. He was a man who smiled a great deal and enjoyed being down with us squealing and rolling and roughhousing on the floor. He would be over at least twice a week for dinner, and my father and he would have great laughs together, bellowing on into the night while Coleen and I, having been sent

early together to bed, would sit up on our mattresses be-
moaning the fate (more exactly our mother) that had seen
fit to deprive us of the merriment and joviality only a few
short yards and a staircase away.

After one of these evenings, on another gloomy and
overcast morning, I heard my mother in the kitchen talking to father.

"Tom is a bum and a wastrel, there's no denying the
fact," said Mother.

"Ah, he's a lad yet," said my father in his defense. "He's
finding his way."

"He's finding a way to keep his fat stomach filled at our
expense is what he's finding," said Mother.

"And he's good company," said my father.

"For you, maybe," said my mother. "But not for me! I'd
be glad never to see him again after what he's done. Do
you know that on top of everything else, the two of you
emptied half a bottle of Scotch last evening?"

"I will worry about the finances," bellowed my father.
"It seems to me I do a pretty fair job of keeping this family afloat."

"It may seem that to you," said my mother, "never having since the day I met you worried about a thing or taken
one step to get ahead."

Then I heard the side door slam and there was a large
commotion of banging and slamming of dishes and silverware in the sink. I wondered then if I would ever see my
Uncle Tom again, or my father, for that matter. And what
was it that Tom had done that had caused my parents to
argue so?

Well, that was only the beginning and as time went by,
the arguments grew louder and worse. Uncle Tom would
still come to visit as he always had, but it was cheese and

crackers mostly, and of course the Scotch, and when the two of them would give us, me and Coleen, the usual huge bear-hugs and wet, liquor-smelling kisses good-night and send us off to our beds, I noticed that Mother, too, would retire up the stairs into her room and close the door while the party continued unabated down below. Father and Tom had tried to keep her downstairs but she would have none of it. Late into the evening they would discuss the situation of the world. There would be serious talking, for a while, but always there would be the outrageous, uproarious laughter at intervals, punctuating the firmly rooted, devil-may-care frivolity from the living room.

What Uncle Tom might have done I couldn't imagine. Murder went through my mind. It was the way a murderer might be treated, if his crime were kept within the family. Mother had said she never wanted to see him again. She had said the same or something similar to me on one occasion, but it was said straightforwardly and with a high-pitched emotion, and it was quickly forgotten. With me it had come one evening when I overflowed the toilet and just left it running while I scampered out the back door without notification to anyone. It was the kind of thing I never heard before addressed to a grown-up. Grown-ups, I had noticed, seldom spoke to one another in that cold, threatening tone. "Don't worry, it's nothing," I had heard my mother say to her sister when she broke a valuable dish of my mother's and it lay in unworkable pieces at their feet.

And once when my thin, mean great-aunt Opal rushed pale and wide-eyed from the hall W.C., badly shaken and moving from wall to wall with the stiff gait of an alarmed stick insect, having just moments before, just as I had, overflowed the toilet, I remember Mother taking her consolingly by the arm into the living room and my father saying to her, "Oh my goodness, I'm so sorry, Opal. I *have* meant to have that looked at. It happens all the time." Even with logs of fresh new feces floating like steamboats and riding on a river that threatened the wood of the hallway, even then they were, grown-up to grown-up, gracious within the scope of any calamity.

So for Mother to call Uncle Tom, a grown-up and a relative to boot, a bum whom she never wanted to see again was to express a sentiment that sounded, certainly to a child of my few years, altogether irreversible.

And so the story continued. And our lives. I entered the girls' school of Our Lady of Lourdes and Coleen started the seventh grade and began learning French. I remember her then speaking in English with that prosaic diction that some young children develop which portends a firm understanding of the way things are and a cool and efficient studious practicality in bending those ways to their purpose. It was well known even then that she was smarter than I. She carried a strange and sullen dignity within her that made me feel at times as though she were somehow above all the squabbles and quarrels that continued unabated within our little home. There developed in her a sort of reserve and it was one that seemed to draw her closer to our mother and at the same time lock out Father from her emotions. Why these things happen, I'll never know. If anything, she had been his favorite. As with all huge men, he enjoyed bouncing the little one on his knee. Me, he would call his "beautiful young lady," but Coleen was the one he would spend more of his pranks on. It seemed that more and more of his jokes were for her, his asides directed always a head below my own. I think now that he was then becoming a little afraid of me. I was becoming a woman, and he knew after all what to expect from *them*. Or perhaps he saw when he looked in Coleen's eyes a sullen judgment and he felt that his attentions should be exaggerated when it came to his little one, lest she be lost to him completely. Whatever he was thinking, this soon became the case.

Mother and she began to talk quietly, sometimes in the small yard behind the house, each cradling a cup of herbal tea, or they would be in the attic together cleaning up and I would hear them discussing Uncle Tom and Father as though they were dead people who had each in his own way and together burdened them somehow with a load they could not, or would not, carry. What it was that Tom had done or why such great resentment developed for Father within Coleen and mother I still couldn't fathom. I was more sure than ever that the secret must be a terrible one, and since Coleen was entrusted with knowledge of it I withdrew from her and Mother almost completely for a time—for a time, in fact, if the truth were on the table, that still exists even after these many years.

The fighting between Mother and Father continued with ardor. Nothing he did seemed correct to her, and even on the rare occasion when he would return from work with a handful of mums or a small plant for the sill, the dinner hour would be filled with a sullen vacancy.

Father and I grew closer in the few years before his death, and the closeness was filled with longer and stronger hugs and weekend walks about the neighborhood with his arm around my neck or his large hand gripping my shoulder. There was very little left of the rum and racket. His jokes and his puns were much fewer now and devoid of the raucous wild humor of the past.

Uncle Tom would still come over, but less frequently,

and their demeanor together seemed restrained and somehow leavened. There were few of the old ballads sung and
these only half-heartedly. Near the end, the songs became
hushed and incomprehensible as if a forgetting or a loss of
belief were enveloping the evening. The heroes of which
they sang still withstood a sea of storm and reached the
shore intact in body and soul, but I sensed a resignation.

At the funeral I sat with my Uncle Tom on the opposite
side of the aisle from my mother and Coleen. There had
been a large brouhaha about this but I would have it no
other way. A fine choir sang from the rear loft: *Dies Irae,
Ave Maria, Jesu, Joy of Man's Desiring.* My uncle stood
in the pew and read some lines from Tennyson:

> Of those that, eye to eye, shall look
>> On knowledge; under whose command
>> Is Earth and Earth's, and in their hand
> Is Nature like an open book;
>
> No longer half-akin to brute,
>> For all we thought and loved and did,
>> And hoped, and suffered, is but seed
> Of what in them is flower and fruit;
>
> Whereof the man that with me trod
>> This planet was a noble type
>> Appearing ere the times were ripe,
> That friend of mine who lives with God.

When he sat beside me with tears in his eyes and his
head held high and his massive jaw firmly fixed beneath
that important red, rough beard, I looked full at him and
then at the coffin that in the center aisle separated him
and me from Coleen and Mother. He patted me on the
knee and he took my smaller hand in his and squeezed it

firmly. And it was then that it dawned upon me what Tom's crime was. It was so simple that I had completely overlooked it. There was no murder, no body buried along the roadside, no misanthropic act so vile as to make Mother hate Tom so. It was that he was a dreamer, a poet, a singer of songs, a man naïve or disinterested in the superficial, fashionable ways of the world at large. And she saw him as the man who had piped her husband into his way of thinking. She saw it like this. But what had really happened was that Uncle Tom had stolen that whimsical side of Father from her, that side of him which somehow or other she had never allowed him to share with her. And so, unwittingly, he had found another to share it with. What Uncle Tom had done was nothing more than to love him better than she herself could know to do.

Bridgework

ast week they told me I need a root-canal. I'm almost
forty and you have to wonder, what's the point? This
is a big investment in a shaky future.

The tooth is not directly in front, it's a little over on the
side, an eye-tooth. It's for ripping and I don't have that
kind of ambition anymore anyway. I told them, pull it out,
leave the hole there. They wanted three hundred dollars
for the root-canal, two-fifty for the post and cap. Or vice-
versa. I told them, pull it out and leave the hole. What's
the point?

They had a big set of plastic teeth sitting up on the shelf
by the X-ray machine. The hygienist gave me a new tooth
brush, a soft. It comes with the cleaning and rays. I always used a hard; that's why my enamel is all brushed
away. She says you should use a soft; it's good for the
gums and it won't brush away the enamel. She told me
"Stop smoking, you still smoking? That's why you got that

brown shit all over your teeth." This is a cut-rate place and that's the way they talk to you. I don't mind because I'm three-fourths dead anyway and nothing surprises me anymore. The priest I used to go to confession to left town with a woman. Everything is changed from when I was a kid.

How the Dentist Feels

One thing I emphasize with my own children is dental care. I live each day within a vortex of abscess, decay, root-rot, pyorrhea, receding gums, etc. I find that even when I'm out with my wife, say at a cocktail party or just shopping somewhere, I never look anyone in the eye. I focus on the mouth. I can tell what kind of person you are by holding a Beefeater Martini and standing in front of you watching your lips go up and down. Are you fastidious? Intelligent? Logical? Clean? I go by the condition of the teeth. This is occupational with me.

In my office, when I am confronted by a mouthful of decay, I send the person to my hygienist in the next cubicle to teach him how to brush: up and down, up and down. With a soft bristled brush, not a hard one. We changed that because people were giving themselves gum problems and brushing all the enamel from their teeth.

My kids could go in the movies with the teeth they have. But I insist that they first finish school. I wouldn't push them into dentistry, but it's a good life. You can play a lot of golf and there's time to travel. Most people pay cash up front or a check. I have my receptionist explain all this to the patients so there is no misunderstanding. Some patients say to me: "I'm too old to worry about crowns and

bridges. Just pull it out. I'm not entering any beauty con-
tests." They don't understand that the *quality* of life mat-
ters above all no matter what your age. I'm fifty-two and
I just bought a little 560 SL Mercedes. This is what life's
all about. You have to be able to look out on the world and
smile without being embarrassed about your teeth.

What the Hygienist Says

What I wanted to be was a hair-dresser but my father said
no, that the next step after that is walking the streets. He
was afraid of all the eye-shadow and rouge. So I went to
this dental hygiene course and I got this job. I make $140
before taxes and I figure I make this guy fifty thousand a
year. Plus I do the X-rays which I didn't even figure in.
My father says, what about his overhead, his heat and
electricity. He tells me I have no understanding of how
the world goes round. All I know is that this is a shitty
job cleaning up all this garbage in people's mouths. I keep
a little stuffed squirrel on the counter next to the chair in
my cubicle and it has a sign on its shirt that says SMOKING
STINKS. This way they get the point. And I tell them, too.
For this salary I don't care if I insult somebody. I'm Italian and I'll tell anybody where to go.

The Dentist's Wife
Makes a Point

In my next life I hope to marry a toothless man. Young,
not too unattractive, maybe a professor of something or
other, but with a private income. I can't see living in three

rooms some place. I would need a few acres and a substantial house within which to entertain, so there would have to be an inheritance. I couldn't live with someone, say in the sixty-to-seventy-thousand-dollar range. I know that sounds sort of silky, but it's a fact and I can't lie about it.

I have had it with dental conventions, dental magazines, cabinets full of dental floss and red-dye pills that show where you didn't brush when you chew them. My closest friend's husband is a surgeon and he makes three times what my husband does, even though he has to wear a beeper.

She tells me they are only ten or twelve major operations away from a Rolls-Royce. She's a firm believer that you need a goal in life to give you incentive. She is very intelligent, having done undergraduate at Radcliffe and adult education at Sarah Lawrence. She has one son, a swimmer at Georgetown, and her daughter, Vikki, is in the gifted children's program. I think if they told us on the news that the world would blow up at six o'clock tonight, they would all be out on their lawn properly dressed and holding hands just to give an example. *My* husband is a major disappointment, but he makes a good living.

The Patient Is Given a Further Opportunity to Express Himself

This Thursday I have another appointment and I have the feeling that after they look at all the X-rays, I am in for a private conference. I hope they don't send me back to the hygienist. I don't think I have one good tooth in my mouth, and I know that the one way in the back on the top is impacted because I can feel it with my tongue. They'll probably have to pull them all. My boss at the Beverage Mart told me I look ridiculous with that big gap where they pulled the tooth. I told him I'm three-quarters dead at least and I don't have anything to smile about anyhow. I just do it to be polite. They'll probably pull them all, I told him. I brushed away all the enamel. I always used a hard tooth brush and I screwed everything up. They taught us different when we were kids. It's all changed now. They used to give us lollipops at the dentist in the olden days.

I would have them pull them all at once but you have to pay before you leave, so I'll have to do it one day at a time. You are some piece-of-work, says my boss. I heard him say some things to the guy who runs the hi-lo in with the Budweiser pallets. Man, he said, he is some looney-tunes that guy in the front. You should meet him. He is some looney-tunes.

I can't understand how some people can revolve their whole lives around something like teeth. People like this can take over the world. They have ambition. They look sharp. They worry about every little thing that they notice. They stay awake at night and in the morning they invade countries.

I was not brought up to believe that a man could chew his way into heaven. But it's all changed now. The janitor in my building today was mopping down the halls. He was wearing designer jeans and an alligator shirt. When he smiled at me, his teeth shone like precious, perfect stones. I passed him quickly, as one passes a wolf or a hungry dog. As I fumbled nervously for my key at the door, I almost said, but didn't: My brother, friend, fellow mortal, those teeth will go. The rot comes on, will have its way. Those teeth will go, as all have gone before.

First Sight

Yakking, yakking, yakko, yak, yak. Blah, blah, blah, blah, blah, blah, blah. Bullshit on top of bullshit À la mode. Everybody in the yolk of the universe had a microphone plugged in and two gallons of air pumped up his ass. Yappity yappity fucking yap. Rader was sick of it way on up to the hairs in his ears. Everybody with an opinion to hawk. Every thimblehead with a neck could tell you how to save your soul, how to win the war. Every gavone with a tomato plant will tell you how to feed the world. Talk and double-talk and triple-talk. Quack quack quack. Quack.

And then Rader, one night, in a dream, saw Jesus. In a car. It was a woman driving, probably Mary. A black man rode shotgun and Jesus was just a baby sitting in the middle without a seat belt on him. Rader was standing on a foggy corner under a pink-hued street light, the kind that saves money but gives you a pink-eyed look at whatever shit be hanging on the corner.

The car stopped at the traffic light. Right next to Rader. That's when he saw Jesus. A gold rainbow thing was happening around his head, that's how he recognized him. Rader moved right up to the car and looked past the nigger quick to the baby Jesus because his eyes was magnetized.

"Say, whatchu want?" said the nigger, moving his elbow off the open window part of the door and moving it inside.

"Salvation," said Rader honestly.

"Ain't got some," said the black man. "Back up."

That was the one dream where he saw Jesus first. Rader always believed in love at first sight. As the years humped on him he began to worry that everything seemed to start falling apart after you did some talking to it. He liked people from a distance, like from across a room or across a half dozen barstools where the women looked nice like they would never argue about money or getting the car fixed or how you never took them noplace good and how all your friends are shitheads. It was nice to fall in love from five or ten yards where you didn't have to hear it. He couldn't decide if he was the smartest man in the world, sort of a philosopher of love, or if he was some kind of a misfit of the worst kind. He picked that he was the smartest man in the world. In terms of what he was talking about. He knew he couldn't do math or physics on a world-class. Only in terms of what he was talking about.

He saw Jesus again, for the second time, in Philadelphia. Rader drove down to the Rangers-Flyers game at the Spectrum. He was up around Broad Street looking for a place to park when Jesus sort of came out of the radio and sat on the hump where the transmission goes under.

"I'm going to the hockey game," said Rader. "I got a

axy. He raised his arms, lifting them out from his sides, and saw to his initial terror that they encompassed all the dimensions of the infinite ship and the thousands and thousands of brilliant moons.

People gathered around him. Johnny Carson was there, McMahon, Rooney, Howard Cosell, Augustine. They tried, one by one, to draw him into conversation, but he wouldn't go. He was too hip now to be caught in that trap. This was a new world and a new chance. He would never talk again except hesitantly and even then only on a matter of substance. Just to play it safe.

Trying to Grow Up American

What do he be?

A. Writer?

Start stealing pens now if you're going to write a lot.

A heavy rain had fallen during the night strong and palling in its darkness having swept along the length of the coast down from Athlone across the sprawling fields of Clare to the sea. Seamus had huddled with the horses in a narrow covert dug out of the sheltered side of a knoll. There the three, in the hours before sleep, looked out on the wet and windswept plain, each dumb in thought except for the raw, ancient confluence of animal and nature.

In the morning Seamus awoke rubbing his eyes from the bright slant of sunlight which skipped in from the east over the wetgreen horizon. The horses were already awake and grazing. He shaded his eyes and regarded the wide expanse of fields half-turned, half still thick and untilled. The blasted work was never done. His intellect, though untrained, and his imagination strong and primitive had for some time mingled with anticipation of something—something he couldn't define or clearly picture, but something nonetheless, something other than the blasted plow and the work and the fields, bloody green and pleasing to the eye as they might ever be. The gear and leather he gathered from the deepest, driest part of the covert and he whistled for the ponies.

To hell with Joyce and Thomas Hardy, and he crossed it all out and started again at the top of the page.

A dog in a morgue
Underwear on a bear
Can be slightly bizarre
With a star upon thar.
Blue bacon and cheese
Can start a disease.
A mouse in a blouse
In the winter could freeze.

And screw Doctor Seuss and he scribbled all over the page and his pencil ripped through the paper and it ruined the page beneath.

Third and two from the back of the zoo
It's the animals' game today.
The elephant said to the kangaroo:

Go out for a pass and if not knocked on my ass
I'll throw the ball to you.

The ducks and the geese
All high-minded beasts,
Decided to . . .

I said screw Doctor Seuss, he said. And I mean it!

Ye leaf suspended on a tree
O nature's bounty stretched beyond
The poet's eye, a plow, and husbandry . . .

Wordsworth? Get bent with Wordsworth.

The tomb, beneath which lay the very man whom I had
first perceived to be the vicar did now—I say it here—
begin to rise and rattle with an eerie shake and prattle,
casting shadow from an anxious moon against the old,
chipped, forgotten stones assembled there by unknown
hands. From that chamber door I backwards slunk, mind-
ful that each rape and skunk balleyed me now, each bat,
each owl, that one lamp carried lit against the moon, all
saw this coward skulk, *skulk* from the horror of that scene.

No Poe. No.

I was gored in the You Es Ae
I was bored in the You Es Ae
I was lord in the You Es Ae
I was moored in the You Es Ae
I was poured in the You Es Ae

Answers: Matador, Me, J.C., Yacht, Scotch.

Interview with the Author

I would like to write a story about a man who has no story. Or better put, a story that does not appear to be a story, or isn't actually a story at all, or carries within it the germ of a story but somehow crystallizes into something approaching religion or baseball. Something that is considerable, meaning that it takes time to consider, but is, after all is said and done, so simple as to look at itself as "doneness." Perhaps I'm not making myself clear. I'm talking here about self-consciousness, the absence, as it were, of the rest of the world—everything, everyone other than the self and then, at the same time, the paradox of self-consciousness as a primal affirmation of the existence of the rest of the world.

I'd like to write a story about what makes America great/I need money to buy things, you know I can't wait./Hand me down my rocking chair./If I go bald they'll plug my hair./Eat it while it all stays hot./Burp on you, say thanks a lot./I have to make my country strong./My MX missiles won't take long./Pickles, lettuce, ketchup— Send it/New England make one independent.

I want to write a novel about a man engulfed in a sea of confusion, gulfed in a confusion of seas, seen in an N of gulfs, fused in a con ensee, enseed in a glun of cons, fuselaged in a con game, fulged in an N/C.

I want an agent like Norman Mailer's

Scott Meredith could get me out of debt
For stuff I haven't written yet

Throw me a party with literary lights
Sell the foreign reprint rights
Norman Mailer and Maxwell Taylor
Carl Sagan, Menachem Begin
Judith Krantz and Walter Lantz
Margaret Truman and Edwin Newman

Meredith handles all the perks
Plimpton can do the fireworks
Michael Jackson's got to sing
Don King promotes the thing

If Pavarotti will go to the potty
I'll mix everybody
A nice hot toddy

Leather wing chair for Alastair Cook
I'll need the weekend to finish the book
Load me up with stuff from the deli
And sell the film to Zeffirelli

My Last Duchess hang on the wall
Look to me like a Cabbage Patch Doll
Trade her in for Gordon's gin
Fra of Innsbruck took her in

Andrea del Sarto
Broke some wind
Picked it up, put it back in
Lippo Lippi stood by frowning
Said: Lookee here, it's turning browning

   Yours will be the heart in demand for a transplant—
   well red and never used.

A Stranger Letter from Albertus Camus

> I'm working with Emmanuelle
> Of late, we've had a sunny spell
> And mother died, but what the hell

> That Arab that I ventilated
> Caused me to be investigated
> Perhaps I'll be incarcerated

The Apology of Socrates
(Plato 429?–347 B.C.)

I'm sorry, all right? Is that what you want to hear, I'm sorry? O.K., I'm sorry. Is that it? You want sorry?

   It's the story of an old astronaut with a drinking problem. Then the woman next door has a married daughter who dies and there are sobering moments near the end. Other things go on in the middle and at the beginning. I liked it because he had a Stingray and a funny way of talking. I would relate it to Thomas Mann's *The Magic Mountain* because of the insight and the way it followed the rules of unity, coherence and emphasis, the three things necessary to give validity to art.

Ulysses Short Version

Stephen brooded, hit the skids
Pulled some things the church forbids
Waxed the rosewood, taught the kids.
Searching for some elbow room
He cut out from his tower tomb
Decided to prefigure Bloom.
Molly's lovers grew and grew
Bloom continued to be true
What in Blazes could he do?

Etc. Etc. Etc.

Old Walt Whitman suckin' on chitlin
Robert Frost's mind is lost
Carl Sandburg need a hamburg
Give up some fries you hog mufug.

If Shelley's here, can Keats have a fat behind?
If Bing is gone, can Hope be found?

Willie the Shake, baby give me a break
Caesar's a palace, MacBeth's doing Dallas
Iago's sangria, Juliet's Princess Leah.

Ezra Pound was most profound
And in *Personae* does abound
Original, inspired work
But the poet entertained a quirk.
Cantos one through eighty four
Baffled critics even more.
Ever since the big world war
They don't teach this dude no more.

C. Helping Others? The World of Medicine?
Without abandoning sweet self-aggrandizement.

Mister Gelb, there are no tongues still. Kidneys yes. Hearts beaucoup. Livers, onions, fibulae, erotica, etcetera, etcetera. All available. People are putting it down on the driver's license. Bequeathments, if you will. Fingers, ears, etcetera, etcetera. You just hook up the nerves, the ganglia, the erogenia, the other stuff, I don't expect you to follow this, and you just sew it on or in, depending.

Gelb imagined the treasures that probably resided within the surgeon's home. He'd heard of M.D.s and their wives flying to Europe and returning with antiques enormous and fragile.

Mister Gelb, in Africa, members of the profession have only recently transplanted a lizard tongue into the oral cavity of a rhesus monkey. I'm talking *JAMA*, Vol. LXXVII, No. 2, October. It looks good. You're worried, right? Listen, I'm not talking snakes. This is a large lizard tongue, woodsy in odor but thick, functional. I'm not talking tomorrow, I just want a commitment. We diet the thing for ten-twelve days on tuna fish sandwiches, gin and like that to get the buds tuned in to what they can expect. I don't need your answer tonight. Tonight, you relax.

LENOXLIMOGESANDWEDGEWOODISGREAT
I'DRATHERHAVETHEM.D.PLATE

> I know a man he pull the tooth
> Mercedes-Benz he toot toot toot
>
> Chinee doctor make big bucks
> Gots hisself a old black tux

Bought hisself a cataract
Two rincolns and some Peking ducks

D. *Can you be a Friend of Nature?*
   With a still healthy regard for the capitalist spirit.

Hello, I'm Merlin Parkins and I'd like to introduce you
to the wonderful world of the American Bovine. Today,
thanks in part to the kindness of the Sudden Sam Insurance people, we're going to explore term insurance and its
effect on the Appalachian Mountain Sloth. These poor, delicate creatures are being eaten in record numbers by the
used-car dealers of the Far East. What nature holds in
store for them and how they are learning to cope with these
mass eatings due to the vigilance of the American Regis-
try of Whole-Life Brokerage Dealers is the subject of the
next half hour that I hope you will share with us.
   Cut down a tree and buy a C.D.

E. *Advertising/Marketing*
   Bullshit in the fifty percent bracket.

How shiny can you wax the floor? How shiny? How goddamned shiny? Wax it. Don't take the shine off. Don't use
dullers. Let the sun in. Optical brighteners. Let it shine.
Shine it up. Shine the frieken floor. Put the shine to it.
Shine the stinking floor, you asshole! Use a sponge mop or
a rag mop. I don't *give* a shit *what* you use.
   I love the way my wife's soap works. It makes her skin
glow. I wouldn't want anything next to her but good soap.
She takes care of herself and that makes *me* feel good. I
feel lucky just to be around her. That's why I sent her
name in. Her father told me: *Make sure you get the good*

soap, start the whole thing off right. I'm sure glad I met *him*, too.

Lusting, leering, letchery. TONIGHT at 8. Be there.

F. Banking
Don't let withdrawal set in.

The American banking system is a canard, said Mc-Duck. It's the bastard child of special interest. Let us take those few quacks whose yearly income runs into ten figures. How much and of what can any one of them eat that would make you jealous? What kind of a pair of expensive shoes could he buy that would make you take great notice? You see someone on the Johnny Drake show with Ed McMallard and you do your jealous thing. To what purpose?

G. No Sense Being Nothin' Nohow
We all meet here after the party.

Dad is a jerk and Mom is at work
I'm a latchkey kid and I watch Captain Kirk

God
Help me with my long division
So I can watch some television

750s on the S.A.T.
Meant a lot to Dad and me
Told the admissions guy at Yale
I worked with grubbers in the jail
Tutored kids until they knew it
That and eighty grand should do it

Can't wait to grow up
Party and throw up
Be a punk and go get drunk

Don't want to die from friendly fire
Say I do say he a liar
Lay by the pool, get my rays
The Lord he act in funny ways.

Play my cards on Thursday night
Drankded beer and had a fight
Went to the bathroom, come on back
Wife's fed up and that's a fack.

Let's go to Geneva and talk to the Commies
They just like us with daddys and mommys

H. Social Work?
    Dig on what your brother say
    He smarter than you, anyway.

I'm coming, I'm coming, Gertz said. But instead, he split
for his cabana, changed into a faded pink Izod shirt and
left. He decided that he would never see Myrtle again. He
could make a living even as a thief, he reasoned, but first
he would have to take the law boards. Outside the club
stood a man who would change Gertz's life.

Got a smoke? asked the man.

Do you mind a non-filter? answered Gertz, shaking out
a flat, dried-out Pall Mall.

Any port in a storm, babycakes.

Are you a guard here? asked Gertz, noting that the man,
though shoeless, wore a blue uniform and a peaked hat.

Nooooo ooo, sweetbabycakes. I be a smok*er* and you be
a smok*ee* in that you be packin' the goods, dig it?

The man lit his fag after much effort. His matches were wet.

I be the onliest one anywhere with this here raggity uniform, the man said. That's a fact, Jack.

He gesticulated with a sudden jab of his finger and his tiny body swayed slowly side-to-side as though he were about to dance. Lemme axe you a question. Where you work at?

Gertz was embarrassed to relate his past circumstances and the fact that he was now considering the study of law. I'm a bartender, he said.

A bar*tender*, sneered the man. You be doin' the devil's work, Slick. You be feedin' sin to the folks. Gertz paused to consider this. I wonder, said Gertz, if I might ask you for some advice.

The man began a kind of shaking dance.

Did you see my man Julius Erving on television? Did you see my suckerman score forty-six point? Hands like a orangotang. My man do defense, offense, *re*bound, jump up and down, run like a mufug. Slaaaaam dunkin' fool. *Slam dunk!* Spend five million dollar a *year*. Moren you make your whole slopsink life. Don't bullshit *me*.

I've left my wife, said Gertz. She's very wealthy and I wonder if I did the proper thing.

Lookeee here, cakes, you think I'm *bullshitting*?

No, said Gertz, truthfully.

My man jump like his ass be on fire. Do you dig them shorts he wear?

The man held the stub of Gertz's cigarette between his thumb and forefinger. He extended his arm and flipped the burning butt into the macadam of the street.

Lemme hold one of your smokes.

Gertz shook loose another Pall Mall.

Now a woman, understand, the man mumbled, be a sometime thang. He struck and discarded match after wet match.

Well, I don't know, interjected Gertz.

Don't bullshit me, the man screamed. Gertz zigged as if expecting a blow.

Hey man, you want to buy a radio?

A radio? No, no thanks. I never listen to the radio.

You want to play cards?

No.

Dig this, said the man, stepping back. He began to sing: My mom gave me a nickel to buy a pickle. I didn't buy no jackass pickle, I bought some chewgum.

Could you dig that? asked the man.

I think so, said Gertz.

The two stood and stared at one another for some time.

You want to buy a gun? asked the man.

No, not right now, said Gertz.

Lemmee hold ten 'til Friday.

Gertz opened his wallet and handed the man a ten-dollar bill. I have to go now, he said, reaching out to shake.

You headed to the bar?

No, I think I'll go somewhere else.

You wish to buy a gun, I axe you that?

How much?

What's on your hip?

Thirty, forty bucks.

I sell you this gun, you gonna shoot yourself wifit?

Yes, said Gertz.

The man produced a small-caliber pistol from his groin area. Gertz handed the man a fifty. You can change this?

What for you need change when you be done shot?

Gertz was struck dumb by the laconic, Socratic erudition of the question.

I. A Sports Figure?

Big bucks here, baby, if you can go in the hole and still make the throw.

> There's a town near Dallas named Irving
> Where the roads are longing and curving
> Griffin's the show they all want to go
> But the traffic's unnerving and merving.

I find that holding runners on is my biggest problem. When I go into my windup, they go. The coach says: Shorten your windup, make it compact. Don't do that big leg-kick thing you do with your leg. Keep your eye on the ball and your body in position to absorb the hit. Keep the play in front of you and keep your left arm straight and your head down and hit the open man. Roll out more. Drill somebody in the ribs now and again to keep him honest. Avoid the three-on-two, the two-on-one. Play heads up, all the time remembering to keep your head down. Hook off the jab. If your opponent thumbs you in the eyes repeatedly or head-butts you to death or gums on your ear lobes with his mouthpiece inning after inning, don't be afraid to ask the referee why he allows it. That's the way you learn. He may respond that he feels these fouls are being committed in a way so artistic or with a charm so consummate that he is loath to express caution and warning. Know your opponent, yes; but know your officials as well. If your opponent arrives wearing a '57 Chevvie over his head or if he carries drug paraphernalia onto the playing field, ask for a ruling. If your research tells you that the head official enjoys bowling in his spare time, make him a gift of a bowl. If he is a raccoon or his relatives are raccoons, leave the lid off the garbage can and *tell him what you are doing* AND THAT YOU ARE DOING IT FOR HIM AND HIS FAMILY. There is nothing sadder to see than someone going to the trouble of doing something out of the ordinary and then getting no credit for it.

> Humpty Dumpty sat on the ball
> Over the crowd there fell a great pall
> TVs in the country in all the gin joints
> Curse the rat bastard
> Who won't cover the points.

> The kicker says
> He can't finish the punt
> Unless he gets
> The money up front.

> The mind's a tragic thing to waste
> But basketball ain't no disgrace.
> 2-3 zone can get it done.
> Mind need itself a little fun.

> Cinderella's coach is waiting
> Will the Federation up her rating?

J. *Options and Futures?*

Make a killing in the market. Shoot your broker.

> I.B.M. to the right of me
> Kodak to the left of me

Xerox behind me
My God, how I blundered
Into the valley of death rode my six hundred.

Give me a stock, I said
Rocket me from the red
Something that's cheap that'll make me a bundle.

K. Law?
  A lie-able alternative.

Oh lawyer boy, the courts, the courts are ca-a-lling
Your Izod shirts are washed and hanging on the line
Your racquet's strung with fine Italian nylon
But your balls are in the trunk of your wife's car.

The Jaguar's gone, she went to Lord and Taylor
She didn't say what time she would return
If she's not back by two, the latest, twenty a-after
The court turns over and you have to skip your
    turn.

Will sheeeee beeeee back in time for you to ge-et
    there?
You have a judge and court clerk waiting by the net
If they should leeeeeeeave before you ever ge-et
    there
Your name is shit and that's a natural bet.

Oh, here she iiiiiiis, she's pulling in the dri-i-veway
The XJS is here, now you can go.
Go get the balls, and throw them in the Li-i-ncoln
O tax free bonds, O tax free bonds, we love you so.

I'll sue you and you sue me
We'll all serve papers
Endlessly.

I'm a legal arbitrator
My Mercedes needs a carburetor.

Medicare, underwear
Blue suede shoes and Fred Astaire
If I fall down and I can sue
Send me to the Fontainbleau

Lime is Harry, Gray is Dorian
Where the hell is John DeLorean?
Fifty agents taped with wires
Found he wanted just snow tires.
Prosecution lost the case;
Jury said it's some disgrace.
Collusion like this just won't fly
Let's drop the thing, release the guy.

His lawyer wants a million bucks.
Freedom sometimes really sucks.

Dad's doing law
Mom's doing wine again
My sister's at Wellesley
I'm into Heineken.

L. *How about being an entertainer?*
   Can you sing that song, keep me dancing all night long?

We were for a long while under the influence of produc-
ers on the West Coast. They didn't know anything about
our music, our New Yorkness. Now that we're back, we

have people who understand what we are all about, our art, our vision. To give you an example:

Old West Coast Song New, NY Song

Old West Coast Song	New, NY Song

I don't know what to do
All I know's I love you.
You make all my dreams
    come true.
You make all my dreams
    come true.
	I don't know what to do
	All I know's I love you.
	Pepsi make your dreams
	    come true
	Pepsi make . . .

We sold out the Garden three times already in NY. In Hollywood we couldn't even get arrested. There's sort of a black strain at work in our music, a street sound. I like to think we're more down than, say, the Jacksons. They're penciled in right now for the really big soda share. When they pretended his hair caught on fire, they got ten million in free publicity. Front page worldwide. That's what I mean by marketing art.

> I wanna wake up
> In a city that never beeps
> And find my hand in the till
> My shoe on the creeps.
> These little town shrews
> Are all in my way . . .

An improper approach would be, say, to see yourself as an egocentric sun around which a primitive world revolves.

Oh yes, the end is near
And may I say in my own wry way
That when I could, I ripped it off
And then I fled
Along the highway.
Oh yes, I did do that
And other things you've heard
Them mention
But don't forget
What could I do
You always knew
I had no pension.

When times were haaaaard
And bucks were few
Where the fuck were you
To help me through?
All through it all
You dirty rat
I sucked it in
While you got fat.

I wanna lay a fart in it
In old Neeeeew Yooork.

I want a Tudor retreat
East Sixtieth Street
Start spreadin' the . . .

Tell Barbara Mandrell—da *da* da da da
Trump's ready to sell—da *da* da da da
One half of *all* of it
New York, Neeew Yoooork.

I'm gonna meet her at a table at Twenty-One
I'm having Oscar *Levant* and *Jack* Nicholson.
The Bronx is up
And the Battery's down.

Look who blew in, Rod McKuen:

New York can be a cruel town
If you face it in the rain
Conductors walking arm in arm
While lovers wait to catch a train.

Opie's drunked up
Andy's on drugs
Aunt Bea's kitchen
Is filled up with bugs

Barney's been tokin'
On cannibus leaf
Tryin' like Coleridge
To suspend disbelief.

Otis at Weight-Watchers
Floyd's always lit
Generally speaking
Mayberry's shit.

It's a beautiful day in the neighborhood
A beautiful day if you're feeling good
How are ya? How are ya?

I write the wrongs that make the system go
I write the wrongs
I write the wrongs

Dallas be the biggest hit
JR's shot
Who gives a shit?

Falcon Crest make my heart spin
Kick the frieken TV in.

M. *The Religious Life?*
   If you hear a voice, ask it for some $.

Had Joseph been hip and on to the fact
That Christmas was near, he might have used tact
By wiring ahead and clue-ing them in
That they needed to stay a few nights at the Inn.

The money raised from this event, after deducting for
the tent, the rental tables, wheels of chance, two tickets
on the *Ile de France*, the garbage bags, the sticker tags,
two on the aisle, a trip down the Nile, three Shetland ponies, one BxW Sony, assorted assessments, will go for new
vestments to the Cardinal in the City to make him look
pretty. The missions will wait 'til the next raffle date.

The Mayor kissed the Cardinal's ring
He knew the votes that it would bring
You give and you get, it's hard to knock it
But why the ring in his back pocket?

Charge cards for Gimbels, charge cards for Saks
The Sears and the Macys all charged to the max
The one that they needed, could anyone doubt it?
"For Christ's sake," said Joseph, "you left home
     without it!"

N. Psychotherapist?
    Helping yourself.

I think what I'd like to do more of is connect. I mean, I want to get in touch with myself. I want to find like an inner peace. I think you can do this and still aspire to great wealth. I think I would prefer to connect, say, with people of an upper level who were into like the same sort of things as myself. And then I would later begin to connect with some lesser people to try to help them maybe to connect with themselves. I would like to see everybody get it together and treat each other as individuals. I would like to see the poor get more poor programs.

O. Hedonist with a heart?
    You got it coming and going.

> Got a house in the mountains
> Got a house by the sea
> My boat's in the Hamptons
> Success by degree.
>
> B.A. from Princeton
> J.D. from Yale
> I'll retire at forty
> If I don't go to jail.
>
> Harry and Edith captured their dream
> Jason, the kid, made the soccer team.
> Tell the ref to go to hell
>
> Call up Sylvia and Mel.
> I don't want to be no copper
> Want to live in Bronxville proper

Big white house up on a hill
Look out from my window sill

Hang a flag on Veteran's Day
Wonder what the neighbors say
Stay there 'til I pass away

We charge it at Bloomie's
Charge L. L. Bean
Brooks Brothers both know
We say what we mean

If you read a book and lose your place
Slap somebody in the face
Be the person you supposed to be
Preserve your own identity
Apologize when you get finished
Family name don't get diminished

P. *Taking a Chance on Life?*
   Probably the very last thing to consider.

Let's sleep on the street
Sixty-eighth and Park
See if they feed us
When it gets dark

Times I know, you feel like crying
You try to grow up
You grow up trying.

Larmer Said
He Would Be King

L   armer said he would be the King of England. That's
        if he could have it his way, if he could be whatever
        he wanted. It was a noble kind of a thing. Some of
the other guys wanted to be Paul McCartney or Al Pacino.
Gantz said he would be Wayne Gretzky. Mucci said Bruce
Springsteen except that he would change his name to Lance
Slick, still do the concerts and like that, but with the new
name. Burrows said he would be the guy on the six o'clock
news, the blond guy, the anchor. I said Louis Lipps, the
wide receiver for Pittsburgh. When Larmer came out with
The King, he sort of dwarfed us all up. We knew it the
second he came out with it. That's a heavy-duty title, King.

We asked Larmer to be specific, to elaborate, just to see
if he knew what he was talking about.

"Fifteenth, sixteenth century, probably," he said. "Horses
and like that. No modern shit. I would probably have a
retinue and hangers-on but I would be a good guy all in

all. I think I would give my subjects food, for instance, if I had it there. I would probably wear animal furs around me so I wouldn't look out of place. And then ermine on festival days. A white horse, I suppose, who would wear leather straps on himself with large emeralds and rubies like the horses you see on the merry-go-rounds. He would rear up at certain times so everybody could see it was the king on top. The people would like to see that. I don't think I'd do wars with France unless it would be an easy win and we could gain some territory for better farming and such as that."

"What about the merchant?" asked Werber. "Where does he fit in?"

"You ask me that," said Larmer, "because *you* are a merchant."

"So what?"

"You're a vested interest. I find it hard to see the objectivity."

"How would you like your ass kicked?" asked Werber.

"You're real brave when you think you're not talking to a real king," said Larmer.

"You *be* a real king," said Werber. "I'll still kick your ass."

"Let's be logical," said Gantz. "He can't be expected to get into the merchant thing. He only was a king for a few minutes."

"Then let him pick something else to be," said Werber. "That's a real fat ass thing to pick—being a king."

I steered the conversation away from all of this because things were getting ugly. "Line everybody up," I said to the bartender. "Give everyone a drink of his own choosing." The guys responded to this with merriment and enthusiasm except Larmer who said: "I'm afraid I can't."

"Oh?" asked Farley, the smallest of us all and a graduate of the College of the Holy Cross. "Ya chariot double-parked?" Everyone laughed except Larmer who walked to the door, stopped, turned, waited for the laughter and profanities to idle and said: "Gentlemen, none of us here has heard the end of this."

About that he was right. He called me up that Saturday. "I can see you at my place at two o'clock sharp," he said. "I have other appointments so I would be pleased if you would wait in the lobby until your name is called over the COMSYS."

I arrived a little early and exactly at two, I heard my name called out of a little screen above the mailboxes. Once upstairs, I was glad to see his door was open because I really didn't know what to say or how to address him from the cold side of a shut door. He was inside, sprawled out on the paisley couch dipping anchovies into a sauce and dropping them into his mouth like Julius Caesar.

"Hey, what is it?" I said, deciding to use the familiar address.

"My good friend." He motioned me to an enoch leather wing chair opposite the couch, on the other side of the anchovy dip. "Please take a seat."

The room smelled of rose hips and ginger.

"I have concluded that I must slide away from some old acquaintances, put a few dozen people on waivers, as it were. Now that it's become public in terms of my true feelings about myself and the king-consciousness flowering within me, I look around and I see things that must be changed. Not change for change sake, mind you. What I say to you here has been not lightly considered. First, a king must be comfortable in his kingliness, must not have to be constantly questioned about his motives. Neither can he allow frivolous mind-golf to be practiced and bantered about by his inferiors.

"Let me give you an example," he continued. "I know a guy who went to school with Barbra Streisand. All he says about her is: 'I went to *school* with her, what's the big deal?' Now he means either one: He knows himself to be useless and wimpshit, so how could anybody who went to school with *him* be any better, or two: How does *she* get all this adulation when any one in that eighth grade class could have done the same thing with a little luck?

"This is why kings, or I should say, princes get educated separately, so they don't have to listen to shit like this when they get to be king. It's one less problem they have to worry about. In fact, it's the one thing in my life I'd like to do over. I mean going to school with all these bumfucks. I should have been sent away and privately tutored. My parents should have researched the thing. The banks have programs—if you can prove you have a kid who's pre-king, they loan you the money. You pay them back when you take over your kingdom. It comes out of the highway funds or you jack up the tolls. You tell your Chancellor of the Exchequer to take care of it. There are ways of doing anything. No problem is too large. Being King has given me insight into this stuff. Little people think little. They get slowed up."

"How does this work?" I asked. "Like if you're a king, I mean."

He raised one index finger to the ceiling and his eyes opened wide. "One becomes a king because it's intuitive with him. One becomes a porter because that is *his* calling. Another aspires to knighthood because he knows that although he *does* possess certain qualities of demeanor and a mild rigorousness of intellect, he however cannot compete on a higher level administratively. And these people are all fine with me as long as they remember that you can't piss uphill.

"Now, I've noticed you're different. You have some qualities that will prove useful to me. And in being useful to me, you might very well find *yourself*. By nature of my kingliness I will be forced to distance myself completely from the rabble. *You* will be my ears, my eyes. In return for this, if everything works out right, you'll acquire some considerable status in your own right. Precedents, you might ask? Precedents I give you: Cromwell, Beckett, Sir Gawain and the Green Knight, Shakespeare, The Duke of York, and on and on. *Not* bad jobs. What do you say?"

"Well, I, uh, don't know."

"Something's bothering you."

"I'm a little concerned about parts of it. Like, where do you do this stuff? Is there a kingdom or something?"

"You're getting ahead of yourself."

"Do I still call you Larmer?"

"Privately, we can go on as usual."

To make a long and very involved story less so, I simply say to you that we did. We went on as usual, except that we hacked methodically away at the underbrush of a myriad of old acquaintances. We began to frequent the theater, we raised dogs, we purchased a falcon. Through our bearing and noblesse oblige, we elevated the spirits of not a few of the proletariat (the polo pony grooms, the falconmaster, the lady who sewed our robes). They felt better for knowing us. Because we stood erect, they noticeably improved their posture when in our company.

"This is a fine country," the King said to me only recently. "It is however, much too large for our example ever to reach to the farthestmost burbs. What we have here is a frustrating calling."

As for me, I feel less responsibility than he. I look out on the morass of humanity and I feel, as I'm sure some of the minor prophets in history have felt. You can't do it all, baby. You touch a few lives, you raise a goblet to the future.

"You're a Prince," the King often says to me.

"I know," I tell him. "But that's only a title. If I could be anything I wanted to be, I'd really have to think about it for a while."

Pleadings

his week, I had a guy who was DWI, a pretty well-known dude in town, caught by a cop and busted for driving while shit-faced. The man owns an apartment building and operates a big McDonald's franchise in Parkchester. Maybe you saw him in the paper two or three weeks ago turning over a check to St. Luke's Hospital from the Lions Club.

With you, I'll be honest. Guys like this are nice to defend because they're good for a quick grand just to get the whole thing over fast. Ever since my partner became a district leader for the party, I get a pretty good referral once in a while. Most of the lames I do couldn't care less what publicity they get and always come up a few Jacksons short on the fee, or totally empty, which is worse. Jesus, if I could just collect what's owed to me the last four years, I'm platinum. My clients never have anything put away for a rainy day and they travel the one-way streets of legal hassles. Lately I'm having beaucoup trouble meeting my own obligations.

It's a shame I have to say this, but now and then I lose sympathy. Like they used to say in the army—if you don't learn to type, you're a target for the shooting gallery. Darwin. Survival and all that. Almost everybody's got half a move in him if only he uses a shot glass of brain-power.

For instance, this dude Cefus is the type of guy you probably wouldn't trust to change the oil in your car. You figure he's *got* to screw it up somehow. Cefus holds a book over on Teasdale. Operates out of an old beat-up storefront just like mine only he never washes the windows. He likes to say he majored in math because he deals in numbers. Like the three horse in the seventh race kind of numbers. Or you're getting a goal and a half with the Jersey Devils kind of numbers. The black community still believes in a shot in the dark. The lucky day. The tax-free slide. They look up. Optimists. They're almost everything you wish you were. And when they lose, they throw a party.

Cefus is a little more serious. Problem is, he's almost white. Psychically. Still trying to amass. To build a territory. You start to get serious in this part of town, the people start to get serious with you. You ruin their day, they ruin yours. You have to laugh or somebody has to kill you. Most every fool down here learns that before he buys his first nickel bag. You don't, you wear a helmet and wait for the fall.

Long as I been knowing Cefus, he's in a holding pattern. He's above the little city and his plane is too slick, too chrome. He comes down, he's a flyer in enemy territory. He can't laugh and he can't win. All of this is so well-known that if Cefus bets a chalk horse at Aqueduct, everybody with his head on straight gets down heavy on the long-shot. He bets Baltimore against the Jets in '69, gives sixteen points and he loses the game *outright*. That very same year, he is laying 100 to 1 that the Mets don't finish in the first division and they not only do that, but they also jump up and win the World Series. He wins the superfecta one night at Yonkers with a 45–1 horse on top only to have the leader's number pulled down for interference in the stretch. A guy like this scares people. This stuff rubs off. You hang around with a guy where you can't believe his luck and you start to do foolish things yourself. Like the time he had this feeling that Ali was going to dive for Jerry Quarry and it cost me two weeks' pay. He has a way of leaning on your shoulder and whispering in your ear like it's only him and you.

"I got the straight skinny from Philly," he says to me one night at the Palomar Bar, coming up at me from behind and leaning on my shoulder. "The owner of the Eagles is down heavy on Kansas City," he says. "He's takin' six points and bettin' against hisself. Jump on this one and don't forget to do the right thing."

By "the right thing" he means I should make a bet someplace for him, too, out of my kick because he supplied the information. This is known as a minor league tout, but watching the game on the tube, I see the Philly quarterback seem to lie down when he could win the game easy. He fumbles twice, once on the K.C. three, and he gets intercepted four, count them, *four* times. On top of this, he gets hit with a delay-of-game penalty in a crucial situation. By the third quarter, I have renewed my faith in Cefus's connections. Although I don't bet the game at all, I see Cefus on Monday and throw him half a yard because I am now seeing into the future like Jeane Dixon and counting stacks of imaginary presidents that will set me free. I am embarrassed to say that I can become as greedy as the next guy when I see a good thing.

So—I have told you all of this to lead up to how I happened to defend Cefus in the courtroom and the terrible thing that happened later. I'm happy to be a simple kind of a person, but I hope by what I have already said that you can see that I'm not 100% foolish.

Cefus gets busted. Public intox, disturbing the peace, operating an uninsured motor vehicle, driving with a suspended license, resisting arrest, assaulting a police officer, carrying a concealed weapon, and possession of a felonious amount of Mexican dream weed. They slam him for everything but insufficient tread and buggery with the commissioner's wife.

By the time the whole thing is over, he asks me if I got my license to practice law from a Cheerio's box. And this after I somehow, by some goddamned miracle, got him a six-month adjournment contemplating dismissal. I got his ass cleaned up, put him in front of an easy judge, and made him buy a Sears Roebuck seersucker with a vest, a real Tom Seaver special. I made him spring for a pair of patent leather Haband shoes and I forced him to get his rat's nest of an Afro in order. I told him instead of getting a hurry-up haircut, he should first get a few estimates.

Anyway, I get Cefus up in front of the bench looking like he's there for the Heisman trophy and the judge gives him the A.C.D. Cefus thinks he should have just walked clean instead of being on probation for six months so he holds up the fee and wants a new trial. I told him F. Lee Bailey would get an inferiority complex looking at how I handled such a rat's-ass situation as his. I should have made him put two-fifty up front, but in light of the rest of the story, I feel bad even bringing the money part of the thing up.

My partner is a tax lawyer and he has all these neat, nice, doctor and dentist clients who only want to have somebody figure out how they can turn a $300,000 gross income into $10,000 taxable. They throw parties at the pool and they invite him with all these heavy-hitters from Scarsdale and Greenwich and they stand around discussing municipal bonds and sugar futures. Sometimes, he brings me along, hoping I'll do some serious listening.

"Bob," (this is my partner) somebody inevitably says, "let me introduce you to Irving Wasserman who owns a string of thirty animal hospitals. Bob, I want you to tell Irv here what you were just telling me about how Ronald Reagan didn't pay any taxes at all that year. Now, listen to this, Irving."

Bob just reels them in like two-hundred-pound tunas. He rented out an adjoining office for his conferences because he's tired of talking big turkey with his clients while mine walk by his desk carrying transistor radios and dance to the disco music.

I'm digressing. Right after I finish with Cefus in court, I have this appointed client who takes his second fall for indecent exposure and endangering the morals of a minor. The judge is *really* upset with this guy as I can tell by him sitting on the bench hunched like a cougar and staring out on me and this crud over the top of his glasses with a flat-out disgusted look on his face. One year in the slammer, says the judge, who is not really a bad guy at all, everything considered, and then he says to the defendant, for some reason he says this to the defendant *after* he pronounces sentence, he says, do you have anything to say to this court, and the stupid prick says, yeah, I got something to say, fuck you and the horse you rode in on. The judge motions to the bailiff to take him away and he stares down at me like I am some kind of corn-filled turd.

Your honor, I say, I beg the court's pardon for my client's language. He motions me with a great swiping motion of his arm, back behind the swinging gate that leads to the audience. For all the aggravation and humiliation of this day, I get stiffed by Cefus and I send the county a set-fee bill of forty dollars which takes them three weeks to process.

What I can't figure out is how all these civil rights counsellors who defend all these poor black dudes make the mortgage payments on their $600,000 homes in Darien and Pound Ridge. The forty bucks for the day is just enough to keep me in beer for a couple three nights down at the Ease-On-In. *In vino veritas* is the one Latin phrase that sticks in my mind better than *lex talionis* or *prima facie* or *subpoena duces tecum*.

Ever since the court appearance with Cefus, his value as a drinking partner has shrunk. All of a sudden, he knows everything there is to know about the courtroom and the law like he's Perry Mason or somebody. You was suppose to say this, you was suppose to say that . . .

Anyway, I'm down behind my desk one day. Bob is twenty or thirty feet away at his desk talking on the phone and looking out the storefront window to the street. I'm listening to one of my older customers talk about what ever happened to Hopalong Cassidy while I'm thumbing through a law book and at the same time trying to keep an eye on the Yankee game on this little TV I keep in the corner for emergencies when in comes Cefus.

He's wearing a dirty raincoat with the collar up, and he has a pair of Foster-Grants on top of his head like he's got eyes under his hair. I wrap up the conversation with my client who is just about ready to split, hand him a folded invoice for fifteen bucks which will end up blowing down the sidewalk when he hits the street, like every other one I've handed him over the last three years, and I turn to Cefus, who has his back to me and is staring up into my partner's law degree like it has something to tell him.

"So what's what, Ceef?"

"Lissen up," he says without turning around. "Ack like I ain't here." He is looking with one eye at the sheepskin and the other at Bob who is still on the phone.

"Might be gettin' watched," he says. "I be at the Palomar tonight. Bad fucking new situation." He turns, flips his shades to the eye position like he is just another ordinary jerk, and makes for the exit, past Bob.

Cefus is incapable of doing anything straight-up. Constant foreign intrigue. A hustler from inch one. I've seen him blow five, six games of pool to set up the next one for the big bucks, and then run the table, all the time with the same Benson and Hedges 100 hanging from his lower lip. I've seen him bet basketball games being played in different parts of the country that are already *over*. You can always find a bookmaker with a broken watch and fool him *once*.

"What the hell did that clown want?" asks Bob.

"Nothing," I tell him. "He's got something to talk about in private. Cefus Leonard. Maybe he thinks you're a CIA agent."

"Never been a CIA agent west of Pelham Manor or south of Ninety-fifth," says Bob. "Might get himself mugged. How do you end up with all these scrambled eggs?"

Blind luck is the only answer I can give him. That and that he's half a friend of mine.

Cefus had a problem at the window. Three nights a week he worked behind the big booth at Yonkers Raceway. All these well-heeled dudes, the owner of Daitch-Shopwell, the president of John's Bargain Stores, the chairman of Shannon Beverages, they'd all come up to Cefus's fifty-dollar window and ask for the seven horse twenty times, thirty times in the same race. Thousands on the nose of one horse, a twelve-to-one shot. And holy shit, thinks Cefus each time, there's a fix in here. How can someone bet a twelve-to-one or a sixteen-to-one horse that heavy? A horse moving up in class five thou after finishing up the track the last three times out with no move at all?

So Cefus would empty out on the seven horse and then he would dart up and down behind the mutuel windows borrowing money from the other clerks.

" 'Til Friday," he'd say. "Get it back to you on Friday. Don't worry about it. Never fucked nobody yet, am I lying?"

And then, just before post time, Cefus would punch himself out as many tickets as he had multiples of fifty. And then he would put the seven horse on top in the exacta with every other horse in the race. And then he would watch and wait for the seven horse to send him some happy. He would watch the race on the closed circuit TV behind the fifty-dollar window. "God," he would pray, "let it be, one time."

And then he would cry. When the numbers went up, he would cry. The seven would come up empty and real tears would well up in his eyes. Could God do this thing? To him? How could it happen?

It happened like this: What Cefus never figured out was that most of the heavy-rollers at the fifty-dollar window could throw three, four grand straight off the balcony onto the cheap seats and laugh. Just order another Johnny

Walker Black on the rocks and laugh with the people at their table about how the seven horse got boxed on the inside, or how he tried to make a move at the quarter pole but broke under the whip, or how he never looked like a healthy nag to begin with. They bet him because he was wearing a green saddle-cloth or because the driver was Italian or because seven was the wife's favorite number.

So, Friday I am zigging and zagging from one court house to another trying to keep four of my people on the street with fines and get another two out of holding up at the Westchester County pen by the weekend. I like to think they'll be out with their families for Saturday. Where they'll probably be, if I'm lucky enough to get them out, is drinking and bragging with a bunch of no-counts and getting into the same routine that got them slammed in the first place. I try to be an optimist.

On my desk amid the piles of affidavits I have to get signed and the subpoenas I have to get delivered by the Sewer Service (the court's appointed messengers of bad news), and the open law books with underlined passages I must get down on paper for various motions, is a stack of messages that came in during the day. Phone calls. Some routine, some of desperation, which I can tell by Bob's bolder print. Call her right away. This guy must have an answer by 6 P.M. Eusabio Rodriguez called—will he be out today? (His daughter's birthday.) John Riley from the D.A.'s office called—did you file the motion on the Jackson case? Can you be in Bx Cty Ct tonight, 8 P.M.?—call Larry Pasternak one way or the other. Loretta says dinner at seven at Rye Hilton, meet her, she'll drive up with the Gerbers, you bring plastic (AMEX). Her car's ready at Exxon, $170.65. See me before you go. Nobody in after 4:30. I'll be back.

The phone rings. There is a large black man wearing paint-stained overalls standing in front of my desk. I hadn't noticed him. I push the telephone's red button. "Yes. No. Sorry, Bob'll be back at four-thirty. Can I have him call you back? Glad to. SC2-8301. SC*3*-8201. Right. No, what has four legs and follows cats? Mrs. Katz and her attorney. That's very good. I'll have Bob call you. Good-bye."

The man at my desk is carrying papers. Bob forgot to lock the door. Yes sir. Didn't see you standing there 'til the phone rang. He has papers to be notarized. Insurance. Check his driver's license, a quick seal of approval, a scratchy signature. That's it. "That's it?" he asks in disbelief.

That's it, I tell him. Nothing to it. He can't believe it can be that easy. He has the same look as most of my people, the look of a man who has always been given the third degree, a man detained, a prisoner of the paper-work merchants he is forced to humiliate himself before when buying a car, getting a loan, preparing his taxes, paying a ticket. Something has to be wrong. This is too easy. He's afraid what will happen when he delivers these papers to the next plateau. He stares down at them again in his hand. "That's it? That be it?"

No charge, my pleasure, I tell him. He pulls a wrinkled dollar from his pocket and drops it among the clutter of the desk. In a fancy office he would feel more secure, more assured that the right thing had happened. He'd rather pay and he'd rather wait. It's more official.

Me and my clients. We dance into the courtrooms together. Like an *Alice in Wonderland* trip. My man is soooo slick 'cause he's scared shit. The judge figures, look at this smart-ass dittybopping down the aisle. All my man knows besides he's scared is that the judge is a fool, jim. And he's right. And the judge looks down on the two of us and he sees two fools. And *he's* right. I have a tough time buying either act and I *know* I'm right. We're *all* right. But somebody is going to take this fall and it ain't gonna be the man in the black dress and it ain't gonna be me. Suffer to be born again. And my man will do the suffering. Give the points and make the bet.

A lot of these guys can tell you about the sixty or ninety acres their grandfathers sold off in Mississippi or Carolina because nobody in the family wanted to work them anymore. Or the ten acres in Alabama they let their cousin keep when somebody died because they didn't see any reason to go back. Big city niggers, yellows, brights, everybody with a taste or a pluck, playing with the boy or the girl in hard times, the heroin and coke that hangs around this part of town like dirty wrappers. And when the lights go up, everybody spreads his junk. It's the way you survive.

They buy every ad the white man has for sale. The Bonnevilles, Electra deuce-and-a-quarters, the big-screen color TVs, Wild Turkey, three-piece suits and crazy hats. Still buying up all the junk the peckerwood pinks gave up on years ago. Chuck has learned it's all a fraud and he's gone about his business making the payments on the Ford wagon or the Dodge van. When was the last time you saw mister whitey with a cane and spit-shined shoes? Mud flaps and chrome magnesium wheels on a Plymouth that belonged to a fifty-year-old white man? Haystacks don't wear no hat. You see it only on the old movies. George Raft and Lloyd Nolan.

My people still trying to sashay through life with a little élan and style. And even after all the heartache and the *knowing* that it won't change, they *still* demand justice.

91

"The Man can't do *that*," they say to me. "He can't tell me move along when I ain't doin' shit!" Their eyes move like wild birds. "No, uh, uh!" they say. "I can't get behind *that*. He *can't* do that."

Yes he can is what I don't have the heart to tell them. The Man can do whatever in hell he wants to. And then he can do it some more. And then he can knock you down the stairs and do it again.

And it's 4:20 and here comes Bob. He motions me into his conference room which is like a neat, colorful dream. Two padded chairs, oil paintings, leather couch. Sterling-silver scales of justice on a fruitwood desk.

He shuffles some papers neatly on his big blotter. "You know that strange guy who was in here the other day, that friend of yours, works at the track, what's his name?"

"Cefus?"

"Right. Cefus something or other. I don't know how to tell you this but I was down at the four-two precinct this afternoon to straighten out a problem and one of the cops told me."

"What happened?"

"This guy Cefus owns the ranch. Somebody blew him away on the street."

Driving down to the four-two to pay my last respects to the paper work on Cefus, I stop at the lights on a hundred and thirty-eight, a hundred and forty-three, a hundred sixty-fifth. Once in a while you get a street named something like Tiffany or Longfellow, or West Farms or Trinity. Around the corner from my office is Fox Street. The only fox anybody ever saw down here was wearing a tight skirt and asking fifteen dollars plus the price of the room.

Down Southern Boulevard and Third Avenue, through Westchester Avenue and Intervale, around Gladstone

Square, the rattle and racket of the elevated IRT, the Five train and the subway, the veins that run through the arm of the South Bronx, keep everyone moving forty feet above or below the street so they don't have to be depressed driving through the boulevards of broken dreams and the burned-out buildings.

Nobody will really miss Cefus. I know that. And his story isn't really much of a story at all. But it's a life. Another life. A life among millions of lives. People who live and try to hack it maybe ten minutes from you. No more than twenty.

So what you do about it is, you try not too much to think about it. You go back to your office and you wait around for the phone to ring. For some poor, crazy dude to call up or walk in with the jumbled, clawing weight of a bear on his back. Maybe after all is said and done, after the eagle has landed, that's all you *can* do. You do what you have to. You sit in a broken-down office with cobwebs in the corners and law books piled on a makeshift case and two ashtrays full of butts and an old, skinny necktie hung on the coat rack for when you shuffle with your cousin into the great mahogany courtrooms and try to explain the fucking unexplainable.

You spend your life waiting for the phone to ring. And every time, you recognize the voice. Your own. Help. Help, it says.

Tolstoy's Son

The Russians aren't beefy at all. This is a misconception. This was something I had been led to believe that has no basis in fact. They are very fair, bordering on gray and physically to the left of medium, on the thin side.

I was in the student exchange thing and I suppose one of their gray, thin, left-of-medium guys was over there at Harvard or UCLA doing the same thing I was doing in Leningrad—shit next to nothing.

I was supposed to be studying literature, but I figured I could do that in the toilet at my aunt's house in Dobbs Ferry, just north of Yonkers, so what do I need Leningrad for except to take a look around, suck on a little domestic vodka and find a Russian babe someplace a nice light shade of gray and a little left of medium.

They stuck me in this old apartment complex that was full of fruitcakes from Sweden, Holland, Netherlands, etc.

It was called apartmenski. Everyone was studying some-thing—Economics, Languages, Law, Literature—taking it real serious like they would be the ones directing the globe into the next millennium.

The first night I found a bar and I made a friend of a townie named Rudi. I told him the U.S. was planning to march into Mexico and reclaim the slums and whorehouses of Tijuana, just as a show of force, to show it could be done. In and out, bang-bang. He said the Russian people were peace-loving. He had never heard of Tijuana but to him it made sense that Uncle Sam would pull that kind of shit. He made reference to the Rockefellers. I told him forget the Rockefellers. Keep an eye out for the Mc-Donald's people. It was McDonald's wanted to feed the world but also wanted them to pay for it.

"Whores," he said. "Sow bastards."

I told him their symbol was a clown—Ronald, a smiling, avuncular figure who carried sacks of raw hamburger meat and soft buns that he hoped to exchange for hard cur-rency.

"Wimpsuckers," he said. "Two-faced slimeshits."

"That's them," I said. "How do you think *I* feel?"

"The Soviet people," he said, "wish for a world proletar-iat government. We hope that everyone can find a common middle ground."

"That's a noble fucking thing," I said. "I believe in me-diocre. I don't know why everyone gets so uptight."

"Nor do I," said he, in a hoity-toity sort of way, if I translated it correctly.

"By the way," I said to him, "could you use some after-shave? It's a perfume. It could help you with some of these gray ladies you have over here. It makes you smell like a rock star."

He looked quickly behind him and down the long length of bar and his dark pupils scanned the area over my shoulder to the door. Finally his eyes fixed upon my own. "You got it on you?"

"I might," I said. "In exchange for a little information."

He, with an obvious nervousness, removed a small metal device from his pocket about the size of a pack of smokes. When he flipped the switch on top, it emitted an erratic cadence of buzzing noises. "They are everywhere," he said. "What do you want to know?"

"Names, numbers, facts," I said. "Star charts, satellitical equations, gossip, dirt from the Kremlin, plans and schematics, pictures of your stealth bomber, ice-hockey power play charts, chain of command contingencies, nerve gas formulations, traffic surveys for fast food location hypotheses, anything that . . ."

He raised his hand to stop me short. "For a lousy perfume?"

"Hey, you can always go up, you can never come down."

"I should risk a lifetime in jails—Siberia—for ten minutes of smelling good?"

Let it be said: These people are not so hard up as the Western press likes to make out.

My first class was held in the Great Hall of Plebeian Learning. It was an imposing structure from the outside—boobelesque and gabled with stained marble and orange, rust-streaked ivory. A giant, thirty-foot-high blanket depicting Lenin's face hung from the fifty-foot ceiling. Under it, printed on a banner the shape of an ad that would trail a plane, was the phrase "Do the Right Thing," or words to that effect. Translation sometimes comes hard because, as in English, there is often more at work than the literal.

Beyond the lobby, the classrooms were shabby and bleak.

The windows were small and the light diffused and hazy, and I briefly entertained the thought that we were all (perhaps intentionally so) being made to feel that we were irretrievably stuck in some long-ago time warp.

My instructor had already begun his lecture by the time I found the correct room. He was discussing *Master and Man* (Khozyain i rabotnik) and the short novel *Hadzhi Murad*. The man was small, perhaps three feet high, but he wore an enormous hat which gave him the appearance, from a distance, of a man a full five foot ten, eleven inches. I at first wondered if I were not victim to some faulty perspective because of the position of my seat.

What amazed me most was the strength in the man's little neck in that he could support the weight of the thing even as he moved recklessly about the lecturer's run.

"That's a tough little dude," I said in the Russian vernacular to the Ruskie at my left.

"He's an enormous talent," whispered the student. "He's Tolstoy's son."

"In my country," I said, "you talk in class, they give you a failing grade. You chew gum, they make you stick it on the end of our nose. It's a form of punishment. You learn from that."

"Is wonderful here," he said, surprising me with his halting English instead of the Russian I was speaking. "I am called Alexi," said he.

"I am G.I. Joe," I said. "Call me that. It might save you some embarrassment at some later date not to know my true identity."

I lifted from my open bag a jar of pickles and placed them on my desk. His eyes widened to the size of poker chips. Pickles are a rare delicacy inside the heart of the Iron Curtain. "This is for you," I said, removing the top and holding up to his eyes a miniature sweet gherkin. He snatched it from my hand and devoured it whole as would a great northern wolf. I screwed back the top and smiled.

"Perhaps you would like the whole jar?" I let him see my teeth. "This would make you king of the discos, no? There's a gray fox out there who would like to share these with you after you've made your best play. These little green fellers could make you more famous than the first chump in space."

He fairly lunged for the jar but I moved it far to the right side of my desk, out of his reach.

"What thing," he asked, "do you want in return?"

"Oh, a little information."

"Is what information?" he asked in English still.

"Charts, nerve gas formulations, anything you can scrounge up. Something valuable—gold—I don't care. Something that you'd think I would like. Use your imagination."

"I, too, have a value system," he said. "You dungaree fuck."

Early in the mornings from the great southern window at the apartmenski dorm, I would look out over a narrow street called Pushkin Plaza. Beyond lay frozen snow, tundra, a snake-like body of ice, and then finally, way down, Afghanistan. Hardly anyone goes down that way. The world lies north, east, and west. Down, meaning south, has taken on a literal meaning.

For the week that followed, Alexi and I would kibbitz in the back of the classroom. He was a third year student at the university and therefore considerably behind me in terms of knowledge, maturity, sensitivity, and hipatudenosity. His teeth were uniformly black and one directly in the front was missing altogether. He combed his hair, it seemed to me, with that typical Slavic sadness that anyone who has even lightly traversed this country will recognize. Had he combed it straight back with a who-gives-a-shit stroke, I would not have taken serious notice nor would mention be made on these pages, but there were pompadourian hills and wretched, fenderous valleys. Low on the neck, where nothing further could be done, a simple brown butcher's string gathered the residue into the tiniest of a pony's tail. His nickname, I heard later, after our horrible altercation, was: *Lechtingraddowsky*, which translates to something approaching: *The Man Whose Main Tooth Has Abandoned Him*. That he would neglect completely his dental hygiene and yet take such meticulous care with his wig gave me pause.

On weekends, Alexi escorted me to Lenin's tomb, the Oxen-Pull Championships in the outer regions, the Line-Forming Competitions of Greater Leningrad, the Museum of Factual Learning, the Young People's Chess Conservatory. He opened my eyes to the wonders of aquatic ballet and we heard Mussorgsky's Great Symphony in the Hall of the Free Peoples. Here it was that we met again the little man, the professor of the enormous hat.

He recognized Alexi and asked both of us to join him for a drink. I paused at this, thinking then that one shot of vodka would surely knock the little man on his narrow, almost nonexistent ass. He could certainly, and with small effort, be carried, of that I was sure, but the ignominy accompanying his being dragged shitfaced into the dipsomaniacal gloom of night-time Leningrad by two of his pupils, I worried, might somehow be reflected negatively in my grade.

I resisted, then succumbed, to the impulse to bolt. I left the two of them there, standing in the Great Hall, each

99

picking at his nose and studying the other's shoes, as is the Russian habit.

That same evening, I dated an American exchange student from the apartment. She was studying Tolstoy, so I took her to a bar on the Great Boulevard of Soviet Literature, not far from the dorm. I had been scrambling long enough for information, and I decided that since the lady was leggy, languid and lithesome, I would direct my immediate attentions to locking lips, etc. She reminded me of Miss Iowa.

"How long you been here?" I asked.

"Two months."

"Ditto." I went to the bar and carried back two vodkas to the table. "You know, we're going to be here a long time. We should get to know each other."

"I try to associate with Russians as much as possible," she said. "But the spoken language puts me up against it."

"It's a bitch," I said. "But you *have* had some training?"

"It's the ear that's the problem. Reading and writing's no problem. I'm translating Tolstoy."

"I thought he was all translated out. Would you believe I know somebody who says he's his *son*?"

Just then I saw Alexi enter by the front. Behind him, like a little walking shopping bag, came Tolstoy's son, hatless and weaving from drink. When they saw us, they came right for the table. Alexi kicked my chair out from under me. I sprawled helplessly to the floor and the little man was on my chest in a flash, biting at my ears.

I thrashed my head about and felt a gnash at my temple, teeth against skull. Alexi was kicking and the girl was screaming. I threw off the midget and tried to regain my footing. "It's Tolstoy's son," I said. "I can't believe it."

Alexi caught me full in the solar plexis with his boot and

I fell again, face down, trying to catch my breath. The little man grabbed me by the hair and was pounding my head into the hardwood of the floor. I remember the girl helping me to my chair.

"Thanks for the screaming," I said to her. "I think that helped."

"I don't have to come to Leningrad to see *this*," she said. "I can see all of this I want at Iowa State."

"I was attacked by Tolstoy's son," I said through cracked lips. "That's fucking unreal."

She swung a WNET tote bag over her shoulder and joined history. I felt in the pocket of my G.I. coat for the pickles. They were still there, the glass smooth and unbroken against my fingertips. The crime, I decided, had been one of passion and not avarice, thus forgivable.

I left and stumbled weakly back to the dorm. It was as though I had scaled walls, dodged flames, chewed gnarled wire barbed. I had evaded dogs, crawled through mud, screamed the agonized lunatic's scream. I went straight to the bathroom, propped myself via hands on the sink, locked elbows, and saw in the mirror a man with blood caking his lips and flowing red down each side of his chin. A wound had been ripped into his scalp at the hairline.

"Nice people," I said to the face in the mirror. "What the fuck," I said to him. I said this audibly because that is what an American would say. "What the fuck." That is what young America *says*.

Honesty

We are, yes it is our generation, resurrecting and nurturing the age of the beast. I speak to you not as a radical Republican (is he such a combination of egoist and blackguard that he would wish down upon us a tidal wave of nuclear destruction?); and I speak to you not as a bleeding heart liberal (is it he who will save us from destruction only to have us each buffeted about in a maelstrom of mediocrity, self-flagellance and profligacy of purpose?).

We measure our months with a time when children write unabashed biographies of their parents and accuse them, if little else can be found, of the felony of good manners.

Early this week, a young woman with whom I was speaking sneezed full-force over the chest of her pale pink sweater. She wiped the dampness away with her hand all the while not missing a syllable of soliloquy. I could not help myself. "Bless you," I murmured, only half-intelligibly, and this when it was apparent that from her point of view I should only have been listening. Was it the elliptical mention of God? I wondered. Or was it that sneezing and farting and belching had become seen, finally, as things so innately a part of the animal condition that they are, since we are admittedly animals at the core, unworthy of comment, apology, or notice?

The story begins years ago, a simpler time perhaps, when one felt less necessity to be blatantly honest to near strangers about one's inherent and inevitable dishonesty. It was a time when, although no better than our own at its base, one could take some comfort in knowing that a proffered opinion of a small stream of talk would not be inexorably forced to trace itself back to some ancient event in one's childhood that enforced in us now a kind of eccentric or skewed vision of things as they are.

"I don't care for large and loud parties," I remember then having said to my wife.

"Well, we don't have to go," she had said. "We can stay home and relax or we can have a quiet dinner out someplace."

Today, this wouldn't get it. My wife of that time has long ago gone, she having grown heavy with deep questioning. "Why?" she began asking a few years after that conversation. "What is it that makes you feel so uncomfortable? Why is it that every time *I* want to go somewhere, *you* find a reason to be so uncomfortable?"

I felt, finally, that I was holding her back from some duty of purpose, from the great, bubbling world of small talk that seemed to make some beings whole, to reinforce in them the confidence of communal mediocrity: the drunken insurance executive who holds his Scotch at his belt and whispers incredible esoterica from the unfathomable world of tax shelters and golden parachutes; the doctor of medicine who, despite heroic attempts, has yet to find a dealership sufficiently empathic to the needs of his classic 190SL Mercedes; the director of music at the high school who unabashedly, after his third martini, breaks into sobs at the mention of Handel's *Water Music*; the interior designer who worked once with a man who had worked with the Eisenhower family.

Frankly, I don't presume to know, or care to participate in, the psychological scrabble of analyzing the component makeup of such creatures. I simply say that they sometimes cause me a bit of sadness; and it is, I think, a sadness born of compassion and not cynicism.

It might be (in fact, it has been) said that I, myself, am wary of any depth of social commitment. I would argue against this if I had the energy. It seems an unfortunate concomitant of the anxious to want to help you find or create your own personal anxiety and share it with them. I see it merely as a search for pain. Pain has had its way with me from time to time. It finds me. I say let pain make the journey and then deal with him upon his arrival.

My second wife is much younger than I. She is a Sagittarian, she is fond of saying. She is direct, forceful, loves to travel, is witty, talented in the arts, and blessed with a natural and deep sensibility, all by virtue of the sun's relationship to something or other at the time of her birth. Jupiter is, I think, in her seventh house, and her moon is in Virgo. I am a Taurus, she assures me, although I am in fact, if one looks at her charts, a Capricorn.

"You are a Taurus," she says often to me. "There is a slip-up somewhere because you are everything that a Taurus is."

By this I imagine she means that I am plodding, on the

hoof, horny, overweight, and bereft of sensitivity. I don't discuss it with her—not because I don't want to know the truth, but because this is the kind of fruitless conversation I find worthless and barren. She is, after all, a woman of great beauty but clouded intellect. I find all of this rather O.K., but were I ever to mention it, I dread the labyrinthine paths down which I would be condemned to travel.

Her therapist is a nice young man. I happened to meet him at one of the large and loud parties which my second wife insisted I attend. He is of the Jungian school, I believe, which has to do with some sort of common unconscious life. He told me that he had planned to become an attorney but that Jung had captured his heart, had made him see things that he hadn't previously dreamed. There exists a great honesty, he said, in psychology in general and in Jung in particular.

While he spoke to me, he picked at his nose, which I took to mean that, since he was an intelligent and otherwise cultured man, a booger in the nose of the new generation was something to be dealt with directly and without embarrassment or shame. Is there a reason to hide behind a *Kleenex*, after all? Are we not, I wondered, when all is said and done, are we not all of us simply cap-toothed beasts who have learned to read an occasional book and to carry small glasses of gin from one room to the next?

My wife, that evening, wore an expensive gown cut low on the bosom, exposing a goodly portion of her delicate breasts. I wondered how far we would go, as a people, advertising this brand of honesty. I saw her for one fleeting moment as a blond and beautiful ape-woman. We are all destined to go back to nature, I supposed, albeit via a circuitous, intellectual route.

When my mind returned to the conversation at hand,

her therapist was employing the most vile and bestial four-letter words to describe something or other to Harry Waldron, our host. Please understand that I am not a total prude. But neither am I one to ramble through myriad bulrushes of scatology to the face of someone I've only five minutes before laid eyes upon. What he was saying wasn't particularly funny, or witty, or well-put, for that matter, but Harry, a senior analyst for a large brokerage house on the Street, was laughing like hell.

"I don't know," I interjected. "I must say in all honesty that I'm probably not a very honest person. It seems to me that I've been particularly dishonest in not telling various people what assholes they really are. I guess there *is* something terrible in my childhood that I submerged that makes me keep it to myself. I'm going to try to deal with that. I've been very selfish in not sharing these feelings and I hope you understand that it's going to be difficult for me and I pray you'll help me along. What I feel like doing right now, after two glasses of gin and an overabundance of listening to the most banal, self-serving conversation, is to vomit, Harry, all over your hand-woven Chinese carpet. That would be honest. But I'm not there yet. It's going to take some time, I'm afraid, to get a complete grip on my honesty. You might invite me back soon and I'll have worked up sufficient real feelings to puke a little bit in every room of the house. I know you'll see this as a real coming-out for me and you won't harbor hard feelings."

"I don't believe what I'm hearing," said Waldron.

"I don't blame you, Harry," I said, as he followed me to the hall closet where I got my coat and hat. "We're all bearing down on a new enlightenment. Let the shit fall where it may."

My wife stayed because, as she said later, she *wanted*

to stay and it would have been dishonest for her to leave. She was upset, of course, that I had been party to resurrecting that cantlet of the beast which had for so long remained dormant within me, not so much because I had said what I did, but because I had run out so quickly and not given the company opportunity to help me go further into it all.

"It was too radical a departure on your part," she said.

"Radical honesty, I hadn't thought of that," I honestly replied. I guessed then that there were gradients of honesty that I hadn't even considered. It's all very confusing.

To make a long story shorter, I simply say to you that just recently my second wife left me for a cellist she met at a supper place that we used to frequent. She was honest about it—about her feelings—which I *did* appreciate. She is, after all, a Sagittarian.

It wasn't long ago that I drifted back into my own rather comfortable insincerity and dishonesty. I suppose it's something that happened when I was a child. Whatever, the fact of the matter is that I *do* have a business to run and two ex-wives to consider who are rather honest and vocal about their need of support.

The Baddest,
Baddest Days

You be somebody say old grandfather dude to little
Nolan Cromwell. Seed it in the eye. The mark of a
man shoe-leather to the stair.

That was twenty year back when Nolan helped old Ver-
non Cromwell deliver the ice. They rode together behind
the horse who pulled the ice wagon. You be the boy that
the light shined on, he said. Got the same red eyes as me,
that's the truth. Independent. You be got the fire. That's
right. Man's a man to make a dollar on his own. Tell me
that.

And Nolan Cromwell cried when the old folks died. And
he cried serious when old grandfather Cromwell was found
one day back some white man's house cold as the twenty-
pound ice cube that was melting up side his old-time self.
Nolan had wanted to drive that old horse to deliver the
goods alone, but his old man had the horse and wagon sold
to a farm in Oxford. Sometime, say Nolan, sometime.

And now here he was. Present-time Nolan Cromwell. Leaning on the front of the jukey box. Make a selection. Select a recording. Pick out the number. That's right. Man's a man to make a dollar on his own. One twenty-one. Take a swig on the bottle of Miller. Stand back. Here it is. *Blue Eyes Cryin' in the Rain.* Willie Nelson. That's what he picked. That's what he got. He sincrotized this old box hisself. That's how he liked it.

Sumbitch's busted say a tall black man lean against the bar. Mixed drink. New slacks creased. Weren't no cotton nigger, nope. Desk nigger. Dark times passin' through nigger. The man don't live here.

One-foty-fo say the man. Mofo's busted. Jus thump, thump. Mofo shit box.

Nolan don't care for no jive-ass up-north nigger. Talk to you from across the room don't even know the man. That's the way they was, jive-ass. Don't make no sense. Never understand no jive-ass up-north nigger.

Nolan feel down side by the belt and remove the clip. Five key. Could be six. One say AMI and open box. One forty-four, he say. I'll take it out. Nolan push the spin button until the number come up on top. Pull it out. One forty-four. Got a thump in the front. Nigger probably deaf. How long he been here anyway, drunk as he is. Got a thump in the front. Nigger be got a thump in his *head.* Nigger thump. Cocaine thump.

This was Nolan's box. From the old arcade out of business in Hattiesburg for two-twenty loaned. Ole Red say, put it in, drag it in the back. Red be owning Red's bar for fifteen-eighteen year. Nolan been drunk six. The end, he say. But Red, he gots confidence. He know Nolan never be dry too long. Good customer. Don't want no re-formed alcoholic haunting out at your bar. Red gots confidence.

Nolan be drunk plenty more on and off.

Nolan say: Red, we split the quarters. You got the location, I got the know-how. You got shit, say Red. Smile. You got fried brains, say Red. Drag it in the back. Put some cowboy songs on the left side and you touch quarter one without me I hit you so many times you think you surrounded. Drag that raggity-ass box in the back and make sure it work fore you plug it in. Business is business. Ole Red move the big green plastic radio from behind the bar and brang it home where it was first. Work for myself say Nolan Cromwell, jus like my grandaddy done. Juke box business. Nolan's Vending Company.

R.C. from the laundrymat say: Nolan, you got a pinball for over by the dryer? Shove it in, man. We make some hay while the wash spin. So, machine #2 in R.C.'s laundrymat. Turn it down, say R.C. Damn bells make me dingy. Jus make the ball roll. No bells. Business is business. Nolan turn it down on the inside. Don't work for R.C. Gots his *own* business. Sole proprietorship, say Joe Willie Washburn, the barber who drawed up the papers. Notarized public. I'm proud as shit of you, Nolan. Drunk as you always be, I never think I'd seed you a sole proprietorship. You got the ambition of a Jew. Caint keep a man down got America in his blood.

Nolan say to J.W.: I got one game on hold. Shame ole Red and R.C. be sendin' quarters down south and you be tap city, smart as you is. It's a pinball say Nolan. Face of James Brown right on top where the score boxes flip. R.C. got a Wayde Newton. Nobody want to be lookin at Wayde Newton. Don't tell R.C. that. He be wantin James Brown hisself.

James Brown outatown, say J.W. Say James Brown and the Flames? Fabulis Flames, say Nolan Cromwell. Roll it in, say J.W. Caint keep a man down with business on his mind.

Nolan didn't like the pinball like he like the jukey box. Juke box you push the buttons, get what you like. *Control.* How do a man throw his money away on a pinball, he say to Red one day. You be so dumb as to ruin y'own business, say Red. You run down y'own customers. *Got* to be a fool.

Nolan look at the record real slow up to the light. Look for a mark make a thump sound. This one record come with the box. Jive-ass Detroit nigger record. One jive-ass Detroit record say thump and the nigger find it. Ain't that always the way?

Big black dude stand right behind Nolan, right up back. That the bad boy? What? say Nolan. That the mofo, yep ye-e-e-s sayd the big black dude. Mofo say: wop, wop, wop. The tall man make his fingers move to show what he mean.

Don't work for nobody, say Nolan Cromwell. Independent. Nigger want to dance, say Nolan to hisself. Payroll stub nigger. Never been an up-north nigger know how to keep his mouth shut. Jus keep yappin and dancin. Never be no independent when all you do is yap and dance. Never get no keys yappin like a nigger.

Sheeet, say black dude. Fuck you bullshit? You work for me, small-time. I be the customer.

Independent, say Nolan Cromwell, eyeball the nigger quick. Big farm-growed nigger. Ham hock spade. Grits and green noon and six went north. Never own a key. Pink-eyed nigger.

Nolan pass black dude, sit at the bar and look at Red, goes: Miller time.

That's when the nigger pick up the stool and smash the jukey box. Hit it what, wham, wham, three time. Glass and dents all over the floor. He reach in the box like a body and rip out the record spinner then the wires. Then he kick like to try to break down a door. Then he turn, pick up the stool and smash the jukey box again. Then he go to the bar, get his drink, go back to the box and kick like a mule backward all the time he hold his drink in one hand and balance in the air with the other like it was a high-wired act. All the time the nigger don't say shit. Here he come back to the bar and sit his fat ass down on another stool. Red walk over, say: Now that ain't right, bustin up that ole boy's jukey box, and he pours the nigger another drink. Red think: Keep the nigger kickin on the jukey box. Keep him occupied. Make a friend of the negro say Red's philosophy. Then he kill for you, like a house dog. Red see the nigger-knocker under the bar by the Coke top. Maybe knock that nigger head to Nashville, Tennessee when he don't be lookin. Maybe not. Long as he keep his feets on the jukey box and off the bar, so what. No damaged done.

Nolan Cromwell think he will kill this big nigger. No rush. He will do it when the sun go down. Stuff the head into the jukey box. Forever play jive-ass notes when you push the buttons. Play: Why did I fuck with Nolan Cromwell, like a Tanya Tucker song. But he don't say shit. Not now. Not yet. Stand up. Fondle on some keys. He go. Gone.

Be drivin Buick Electra deuce an a quarter. Humpback whale. Six mile to the jug and ain't that a kick in the ass. Be hangin up this rag don't nothin loosen up. Nolan say, how the fuck a man like me be the wheel of a K car piss ant? R.C.'s laundrymat say: Small businessman, Nolan, need a practical rag. Pick-up truck or a Toyota half-back. Put them machines in the back. How do a man drive a porthole Buick when he gots pinballs and juke boxes to jackass around? Man got to learn what's what to create a business. Mos business fall down the first week an you can look it up. Man take all the long greens and buys hisself a turrible purple suit or a ghetto blaster from the Lafayette store in Fayetteville. Now how that look to the small businessman association? How that look to the chains of commerce? Whitey say, poor nigger. Be but one purple suit in all Mississippi and the nigger bought it up. Ain't that just like a nigger. Ho ho. They laugh like a mofo. White folk think the nigger be here for the comedy show.

Richest man in the world be drivin a jackass rabbit, no radio, 700 mile to the fill it up. *E*-conomy, that's what.

Who in hell you rootin for anyways, say Nolan. Nolan raise his hands in the air and wiggle his fingers like a prayer fool. You talk like a man with a paper asshole. I never been knowin what you be talkin in fourteen years. Some dumb fool kick in my jukey box, bus my income like a kickin mule and you crazy talkin bout no purple suit. I be lookin like a purple suit to you?

E-conomy, that's what, say R.C. I got two dollar, what do I do? What *do* I do? Suds, that's what. Or a mat for inside the door. Or an extended cord for the fan for to make the customer dry. *Business*. That's what drive me. Prettifying things. Customer feel easy, say: Let's go see R.C. whirl some laundries. That's right! How the fuck you think I got in the Rotaries? With ole mats and no fan? They be only two negroes in the whole club, me an Beeze Exterminator. Only two pillows of the black community. Ain't that enough to make a growed man cry? An I thinked you was comin up. Shit, you a dirt farmer, Nolan jus like you daddy first. I puts my profit right cheer back in the business. Make it grow.

What I did to you, ask Nolan, now walking up and back,

up and back. You be only a laundry jerk. Stand up the
floor watch the suds spin like monkeyshines. That be no
big time shit.

Big time shit? Big time shit? I buy you and sell you to
the slave ship, say R.C. I own you like I own these raffity-
ass washer machines. But you come with a turrible, evil
mouth. An *I* put you in business. That's right. I must be
crazy.

Mus be, say Nolan. R.C. walk to lotions table slow. Call
me crazy, nigger? Call me crazy? Now R.C. *be* crazy. Eyes
all fucked up. Mean R.C. R.C. grab fold up chair say R.C.'s
Laundrymat in Magic Marker and run to pinball machine.
Lights flash. Wham. Bang two time. Nolan try to come
from behind but R.C. swing out, say: What? What? Watch
this. Crash. Glass all sprayed out. Boom. Hey, hey, hey,
say Nolan. Hey, hey? say R.C. Hey boom. Hey wham.
R.C. swing chair at Nolan's nose bone. Whish. Then throw
the chair at Nolan, lean on wall and kick over pinball. Oh
shit, say Nolan. Oh shit, say Nolan. Oh shit? Kick in wood
on side what say: Wayde Newton Las Vegas pinball twenty-
five cents. Nolan say to hisself: I'll kill this nigger tonight.

Now, call the sheriff, say R.C. Call that narrow-ass dumb
shit sheriff. Maybe he be up to the Rotaries. Dial the man
so's he can lock your black ass up. That's right. One night
they be twenty-seven Rotaries at your front door with a
rope. Use my phone.

Got to kill you for that, say Nolan. Not now. No rush.
A man got to kill you for that shit. Nolan back to the door.
I ain't cleanin that up, say Nolan. Nope. I *might* be back
with iron.

Nolan do be had some respect elsewhere. Not R.C. Not
ole Red. Washburn eat shit. Been knowin him too long.
Familiary breed condemn. No shit. Nolan drive down

Brother Bear Street to Elm, then left. Nolan R. Cromwell say to hisself: I be a ruined mofo. Four machines to the world an two be busted up. Two be in need of bury-up is a fact. Two stone wreck chopped. Fired wood. Refutation be shit down bottom too when this get out. Nolan should stab three peoples dead now and drive to Atlanta where there be six million Buick portholes with a nigger behind the steer of every one smilin out the wincheeld. Like Charlie McCarthy. What?

Down Elm to Fox. Lean-to burned up chartown. Raggity no hope sad time streets. Nolan Cromwell be called "uptown" as nickname. Childrens be lined up for to see Nolan shake up the dirt with his 225 Buick. Say blueblop, blueblop from glass pack mufflers. Say blueblop, blueblop, real slow, like gliding-by time.

Roll down Fox like President Roseyfeld did once way back from Baton Rouge. Sayed to the Vice President, sayed: Drive me down them honkey tonk raggity-ass streets where the black man dwell. Somebody must carry them to the polls. Notify the olderman. Find me a distrik leader and kick his ass good.

Now Nolan wave with reservation. Not too cute. Old-folks on woodrot porch say: Uptown, Uptown comin through. Uptown come to empty up the machine. Old time dudes shake a head, say: Dam gold Buick shine like a light bug. Goddam.

Nolan park his 225 in front of China Shack Grit Shop. Hand drawed sign in window say: *Chopped Sewey, White on Rice. Tables on the side for private raps. No cover. No minimum.* This be Nolan's number one China dude. Fat man Cholly Chan. What's what, Cholly Chan? Nolan slap five with China man and five back. How you do Eyetalian man? say Cholly.

Cholly think Nolan be mafioso with juke box company. How do you do, racket guy? Nolan can move inside some respect he got downtown. Not like Fred and R.C. and all the lames up top.

How be Elton John swallow up the silver plate? Nolan look to Elton John pinball in dark corner nearby shrimp roll hot tin. Best I call the Pinkeyton truck Cholly Chan. Got a gun? Be here one week, seven day, Cholly Chan. This sweet box help you business like a rag on fire. Pull them peoples in. Like a home bake cake. Lock the wood and get a gun. Nolan drag a chair up next to Elton John dopey face with notes pained on the side.

Wh-a-a-at? N.C. face drop when he turn key and open up cash box. Inside be clean and smooth like a Cadillac salesman. Empty. Nolan slide out the cash box and see in it for long seconds like a hungry man. Caint be, he says. No joke, Cholly Chan. He look at China Man suspicious, one eye up, head lean. What say, Cholly Chan? Play the game on the juke box man? Cholly Chan got the key? Cholly laugh and laugh and have to sit down. No joke, racket guy say Cholly when he stop laughing. Is not play. No chimp-chump play shitass game like that. Kid say Pacmans, Pac-mans. Kid say shit on shitass game.

Nolan look at Chinaman funny. Say: You *might* get blowed up. Chinaman laugh and laugh. Nolan say: Dead China Cholly Chan look funny inside a hole. Might have to send for a China preacher all the way to China. For to bury the dead.

A ha ha ha ha ha. Chinaman get up from chair an hold belly. A ha ha. Then he look bad. Say: Nobody play shitass pinball game. Peoples buy eight egg roll in month. Two egg drop soup. Pint. Four chicken chow mein. Three cat dinner. In month! How you think they play shitass pinball game? Cholly Chan not even pay rent. Pretty soon he pick cotton balls.

Nolan Cromwell slaps on the Elton John glass top then head for the swingin door. His mind say: Never no more trust no China man an no Japan dude. Say to China man, say: Might come a Chrysler New Yorker roll by with machine guns. Soon. I don't know. Might get the order to burn down the whole town. Don't know yet.

Nolan head back uptown in the saddest, the saddest of times. Gived up the sweet life for this business. Sacrifice evathang jus to keep the good name. And now he gots to kill three chumps an a China man. Else hang out on North Avenue with a wine bag.

Think about the small businessman loan but necessary to need R.C. and J.W. to fill it out. Have to pick tobacco in Virginia first fore ever to speak to R.C. again. Might have to cut R.C. anyway or bomb him up jus to keep hisself cool.

Now what? Nolan push the porthole Buick up out past the city. Think of what his grandaddy say to him one long time ago on the ice truck. A sad day when you can't make a dollar. A sad day for the working man. And it's the baddest day of your life know Nolan now as he pull up front of the old two room and turn off the key. It's the baddest day of all when you grow old to know it's true.

Better Bars
and Gardens

So then what happens is: There's nothing. And I mean *nothing*. Tending bar Friday nights at Bellucci's across the way from the college, trying to get the Honda started in the ice, watching the Knicks on Channel Nine.

I said to Bellucci, not that there was anything in it for me, but I said to Bellucci something like: "Why don't you change the name of this broke-dick place and get some college kids in here to drink beer? Put some *music* in the box instead of that Jerry Vale shit. Throw a pin game in the corner. They got nine thousand kids across the street looking for a pitcher of beer and a Springsteen record and you got this dopey broad over in the corner with a fifty-dollar piano and a Blossom Dearie voice."

So then, when Bellucci hears enough, he goes: "Take a hike," which means get gone and don't come back. When you know Bellucci three minutes, you know how to read between the lines.

"Pack it in your kazoo," is my reply as I unhook my poncho from the nub and hit the door. With Bellucci, it's safer to trade insults from long distance or refrain altogether. Big as he is, you can't tell where the fat leaves off and the muscles begin.

"I'm leavin'," I said as I stopped by the open door. "I quit. I *won't* be back."

He turned. His face fell slack. His jaw dropped and his mouth sunk open in mock surprise. "Trow a party for yourself."

That was the last time I saw him until later when I had to ask him for the job back.

II

Weinrhoder got rich somehow, trading fat-backs and rat-tails on the commodity exchange. He'd buy them when nobody wanted them and sell the rights when the scarcity set in. He sits around the bar a lot and sucks on limes that I float for him in a glass of gin. He says this is the only country in the world where you can get on a train and leave town without checking in with the authorities. "It's still possible to become a millionaire here," he says, "as long as you don't file any taxes." He bores the shit out of me really, except that I figure if a dumb fart like him can make it, there's still room left for me.

III

Zeidel is a weightlifter for Barbell City, down three blocks. He'll show you how to ride the stationary bicycle and how to row on the rowing machine. They pay him for this with a cardboard, computerized check from the home office, which I take from him on Friday nights and turn it into about twenty bottles of Lite beer from Miller and then I give him the change. He told me how, although he is Jewish himself, he questions the Jew. "Too much emphasis on affairs of the mind," he says, "to the neglect of the body. A healthy body and a healthy mind are one and the same. To neglect the body is to squander a valuable inheritance. Kill the body and you kill the head."

He told me the only thing he hates more than a phony intellectual is an underdeveloped pair of biceps or a man who didn't know where his next meal was coming from.

"Straight A's," I told him. I think you touched on something right there. He tries to be friendly, but on Friday nights I started wearing long-sleeved shirts. "What some of these stick-necked intellectuals need is a good beating," he said to me one night. I'm not an intellectual but when I'm working behind the bar and everybody gets drunko, I could be mistaken for one, and I'm truly on the cusp of being a stick-neck, so now I hang down the other end of the pine when he comes in, visiting only when he bangs his empties on the hardwood.

IV

Craven owns the lamp store across the street. "I'm sick of dealing with the public," he says. "I'm sick of all these mealy-mouthed mutts who want something for nothing. One day I'll set a match to the whole goddamned thing. I don't care if the whole frieken block burns down."

V

Loughlin drives one of those beverage trucks. One night when Jesse Jackson comes on TV, Loughlin takes his high-ball glass and heaves it at the screen and cracks the god-damned thing. Everybody ducks like it was a bullet until they realize it's Loughlin again. "I hate that sonofabitch," he says. "Don't worry, I'll pay for the damages."

VI

Mister Gwynne is a banker. Branch manager. Steps in, has a few. Brings in a girlfriend from the bank now and then because nobody in here gives a shit. Told me his wife goes to Colorado in the winter and Miami in the summer because she loves the intensity of the seasons. I used to give him a *lot* of buy-backs, like on the house, as long as Bellucci was gone. We talked politics: El Salvador, Nica-ragua, Brazilian monetary policy, Third World stuff. Soft-ening him up, letting him sound important. Then I bang him for the loan. All I wanted was a car, not eighteen rooms in Trump Tower. "You think you could get me a car loan?" I ask him. "I can get it anywhere, but I figure, you're a customer, I'll throw you the business."

"Oh no, no," he says. "I don't handle that stuff. I don't do anything under half a million and even then, only cor-porations, business loans."

I told him, loan me half a mil, I'll give you back four hundred ninety-five right there at the table. I only need a used shit-box that starts up in the winter.

"Wish I could, my boy," he says. "It's just not within my bailiwick."

Later I see him downtown one day squeezing his fat ass out of an eight-year-old Chevvie and I realize he's broker than I am. From then on, he pays for his *own* drinks and I give him the cold shoulder. One Friday night when Zeidel is good and drunked up, I'll whisper in his ear that the guy Gwynne down the end of the bar in the suit thinks you're a fag.

VII

Stephen floats in on weekends to listen to the broad with the Blossom Dearie voice. He's into interior design and I think he's got his eye on Freddie, the other piano player. Stephen wears these tight slacks and a Byron shirt, close at the wrists and billowy in the sleeves. One Friday he asks me if I want to go on a Sunday picnic with him in his MG. I told Bellucci: Get rid of these gay blades or pretty soon they'll be dancing naked on the bar. And that includes Freddie.

Bellucci says Freddie is an artist and he comes cheap. Stephen drinks margaritas and pays cash. "Besides, he's a fashion designer, that don't make him a queer."

"Maybe," I tell him, "he'll write this place up in *Better Bars and Gardens*."

VIII

Bellucci teaches a real estate course two nights a week across the street at the junior college. He snuck in there

122

through somebody he knows when nobody was looking. I guess it proves he *does* have that degree from St. John's like he says, but it forebodes bad times for his students. If the kids' parents ever got a look at Bellucci's expertise with real estate, they'd send their punks into the *army* for training, like in the old days.

I can only imagine this pile of mashed potatoes teaching somebody about floating mortgages, prime rates, equity-income ratios, etcetera, when he not only doesn't own a piece of real estate himself after forty-six years on the earth, but is even four months behind in his rent on the bar, and (he brags about this part) he hasn't filed a tax return since '76. So much for higher education.

IX

So Bellucci takes off for FLA in February like every other bar owner in the world. He goes down there to Lauderdale with his shit-eating Bermuda shorts and thirty pairs of socks, the shoes on his feet, three pairs of underwear, one blue Izod shirt, one green Izod shirt, one BELLUCCI'S BAR AND LOUNGE T-shirt and a green plastic-peak half-hat with a band around the back.

He meets the other bar owners from New York and they bounce around the cocktail lounges with their shorts and their socks and their brown shoes. They throw around tips like a gang of Babe Ruths. The biggest tipper in the world is not a Rockefeller or a Getty. He's a bar owner with a load on. When he's up and around and sober, he won't give you the fuzz off a tennis ball, but put a shot of Jack Daniel's in front of him with a beer chaser and he'll donate his liver and eyeballs to science. He'll leave a day's pay on the bar on the way to the next bar. Don't ask me why, that's just the way it is. It's traditional and the ginmill jockey who thinks he can do it differently is either new at the job or he will soon find himself a new occupation. It's quick clear to everybody that he doesn't belong.

Anyway, Bellucci does the wings of man and here I am, Undersecretary for Barroom Affairs, left in charge. Face the nation. *Shit*-face the nation. The Honda's fuel pump is shot and the exhaust system finally rotted its way into Japanese heaven. It's parked down on Chauncey and Jerome with a flat left rear. I think it has finally lost its will to live. It shows no interest and fails to recognize me. The headlights and grill are covered with frozen mud and somebody snapped off the aerial. One windshield wiper is in the up position, the other is gone altogether. Bleak city is the ditty. At this point, a smart guy realizes that, bad as it might be, it could be worse. You never know when there might be a nuclear exchange.

X

So, while Bellucci is gone, I devise a little plan, a merchandising ploy to put the place on the map. The method right now I'm not prepared to reveal because I'm truthfully thinking of taking this concept public and franchising it again and again around the world. *International*. Five days didn't go by from its inception to the point where there were lines of people literally out into the street, trying to get in. Even the regulars, Weinrhoder, Zeidel, Craven, they can't get in anymore. It's too packed.

When Bellucci comes back from Sun City, he can't believe his Italian eyeballs. He shoulders his way in, bull that he is, by bogarting his way past the people in front of the line. He muscles his way to the bar and ends up with his head between these two old broads who do Amaretto and are here now almost constantly since about two days after I inaugurated my innovation, my master-stroke. Einstein would probably like to talk to me about this.

Bellucci, with his arms around the two old babes, leans up real close to the bar where he can get my attention. His eyes are wide and white, his nostrils flaring with excitement. "Kid," he hollers, "this is incredible. There must be two hundred people crammed in here and another hundred and fifty outside trying to get in. It's a *zoo. I love it!*"

"Go home," I tell him, loudly. "Give me one more week and I'll have this place floating. I haven't even *started* with my marketing. This place will be more famous than the Lido. Remember the Peppermint Lounge? Don't make me lose my chain of thought."

"No, no," he hollers. "You do it! You do it, kid!"

"I can't have nobody bothering me," I tell him. "You go home. Come back in a week."

"Right," he says. "Right. I'm goin'." He looks square at the two old broads from one to the other. He's got a grin on his face like the cat who swallowed the canary. "Are you ladies enjoying yourselves?" he shouts.

"Oh, yes," says one. "We adore the place."

"Great, great," squeals Bellucci. "I love it!"

People are clamoring up and down the bar for drinks. Others are fighting their way from ten deep to get to the pine. "This is the owner," I say to the ladies.

"How nice," says one, the smaller one with the glasses. "We're here all the time, every chance we get. Your bartender is a wonderful young man."

"The best," screams Bellucci. "The best!" He's smiling like a whale, his lower jaw open, his bottom teeth exposed, his tonsils dancing like Astaire and Rogers.

"We've been coming here for over a week," says the gray-haired, fatter one. "And he hasn't charged anyone for a drink *yet*."

XI

So then what happens is: There's nothing. And I mean *nothing*. I said to Bellucci, not that there was anything in it for me, but I said to Bellucci something like: "Get bent." This is after he fires me. I told him, don't think I'm going to do the Billy Martin thing where you hire me back and forth every time you get in a jam. Once I leave, that's *it*.

"Take a royal hike," says Bellucci. "I'll put my size twelve so far up your ass, the inside top of your head will read CAT'S PAW."

That's the way he feels about it. Enough said. Some guys are afraid to spend a little money in the interest of promoting their business. Johnson's Wax spends maybe twenty million a year getting their name in front of the public. Bellucci's brain curdles at the thought of a few short beers that don't immediately translate into the coin of the realm. This is why the Johnsons are waxing the shit out of the Western world and Bellucci is all out of roach spray.

XII

Three days into the off-season and Zeidel and Loughlin catch up to me. "Let's go," they say. "We're takin' you out for a few golden drafts."

"Oh, what's the use?" I say. "Everything falls apart. That's the way it goes. It's entropy. It's Einstein. It's the quantum factor."

"Your *ass* is the quantum factor," says Zeidel. "All of a sudden you're a smart guy?"

"Shit no," says I, lying. "It's just that everything I got is broke, me included."

"Hey," says Loughlin, "you're with *us*. When you're with *us*, you don't *go* to your pocket. There's people waitin' for us. We got orders."

Before you know it, we're across from the college and I'm being dragged into Bellucci's. Craven is there in the corner. With Weinrhoder. And Gwynne. The big tub of whaleshit, the owner himself, is there, sitting at the same table, the wrong way on a chair with his eggplant forearms crossed over the top. He's lecturing them like he's John Kenneth Galbraith.

"Here he is," says Weinrhoder.

"Bring him over here," says Craven.

"Sit him in the chair," goes Bellucci.

"We thought we was friends of yours," says Zeidel from behind, where he's got his claws dug into my trapezoids.

"You are," I say.

"You ran out on us," says Gwynne. "I told you I *can't* give you a loan. It's the bank, not *me*."

"I didn't run out on nobody," I say. "I was three feet in front of a size twelve. That's not *running-out*. That's *flight!*"

"So what are you gonna do?" asks Loughlin.

"Live in my car. Lose a lot of weight. Finish up school. Get the goddamned BBA and get done with it. Don't worry about me. Two years and I'm on Wall Street."

"Wall Street your ass," says Zeidel.

"It's like this," says Craven. "Mister Bellucci and us, we

got an understanding. *You* don't work here, *we* don't drink here. And that's not Humpty-Dumpty talking. Who's talking is five right-down-to-the-wire alcoholics. Mister Bellucci here, he sees you in a new light. He wants to give you your job back. Like a manager's assistant while you finish school."

I look at Bellucci square-on. "That right, fat man?"

He hesitates five seconds to get his Italian temper back in the box. His eyes open up wide and he starts to chew on his tongue. "I'd like to have you back, kid. It's not that these guys spend a few hundred a week in here, neither. You got good ideas, you just get carried away a little. Just *ask* me before you do something crazy next time. Make me feel like I'm important. By the way, you get to Wall Street, call the boss a fat man and see if he's as nice as me."

"You guys are all right," I say. "It's nice to be wanted."

And it *is*. Yeah, it can hold you back from a lot of things you should be doing, but when you add up all the columns, what the hell else is there in this narrow-ass little life that makes a lot more sense than that. What?

Lawn City

Einstein spoke to it: There exists a thin line separating creativity and culpability. Grunwalt knows this as do many of his neighbors, myself included. We live, after all, in Lawn City. Probably the highest per-capita, cash-in-hand town in the entire world. I include the Third World, the eighth world and the newly emerging nations that people in Washington like to speak about.

When we find a creative person, we find him very busy creating money. More delicately put, in creating its diversion, as with a river, nudging its drift. There is but one end to the religion of creativity: Green.

We are not knocking it, you and I, as I see it. We agree on that. We don't knock it. We understand it. We are, after all, both from Lawn City, are we not? Of course we are. Or we wouldn't be talking one to the other, at least not at length. Something special exists between us, something, well . . . mystical. Am I going too far? It has long been my feeling that there is more at work here in Lawn City than money.

Grunwalt is, of course, a doctor. A podiatrist. Which has to do, correct me if I'm wrong, with the feet. His office is in Yonkers, so that you can see that his days are not altogether pleasant, or not so pleasant as they might be were he practicing under different circumstances. His patients' feet, feet which shlep the mean streets of Yonkers, cannot be fairly compared with the fragrant and manicured feet one might expect to find in Lawn City or in Scarsdale, or even Bronxville, for that matter.

Grunwalt drives one of those little silver Mercedes four-fifty somethings each morning down the sun-filled Merritt Parkway which becomes the Hutch and then somehow, making swerves onto the Cross County, turns off into a foggy and rather desolate area onto the Sprain Brook and then you're in Yonkers.

Sadness, like a barnacle, attaches itself to this story. Everything, after all is said and done, has its sad side. If you spin the crystal prism of a fine man's life slowly enough in the clear light of retrospect, you will always spot that dull, etched, cloudy facet. Are we any different, you and I?

Grunwalt's sadness began, as has so often been the case, with a tax audit. Money was involved. The sign on the wall above his receptionist's desk, the one which read PLEASE PAY CASH, was the thing which drove the IRS man, mole that he was, sixteen-thousand-dollar-a-year graduate of a community college that he was, deep into the faint green lines of Grunwalt's accounting ledgers.

What about this and what about this, is all the man kept saying. Over and over again. This is how Grunwalt tells it. How do you live in an $800,000 home in Lawn City?

How does *anybody* live there? countered Grunwalt. But you have an adjusted gross income of $12,500 said the tax man. And what about that sign that says PLEASE PAY CASH? There are no cash entries. No cash deposits.

I work here in Yonkers, answered Grunwalt, because it is here I am needed. I collect very little money. I am owed great sums which I will never collect.

But what about the home in Lawn City? asked the man over and over. What about the house? Your property taxes alone are over nine thousand dollars a year.

I borrow money to pay my taxes, Grunwalt explained, honestly and simply.

There exists a green line. I'm sure you have heard of this, stated the man. And you have crossed it. Stealing is one thing. Everyone has a little larceny in his heart. But you have become a hog about this. You they won't believe down at the office. You are a hog to beat all hogs. You have taken a great deal and left very little.

Grunwalt, although honest and sincere as the next fellow, was at a loss for words. He had majored, after all, in Science, not Literature. Not Public Speaking where you do a double two-step and a ring-around-the-rosey and leave everybody admiring your footwork, thinking you have answered the question.

There was little he could say. The two men stared deeply into each other's eyes. Silence happened between them. And then Grunwalt spoke only these words, the only words that then came into his mind. He didn't mean anything by it. It was something he had been saying every day, every hour, for twelve years since he graduated from the East Side School of Podiatry: Please be seated, he said. And remove your shoes.

The man did as he was instructed, and here follows an

almost unbelievable and fantastic tale.

And the socks too, said Grunwalt.

And then, as the man peeled his hose from his kicks, Grunwalt reached out in the most suppliant manner and caressed the tax man's right foot. He manipulated the toes. Slowly, starting from the smallest and working his way to the largest, he knowingly massaged each pedal digit. He restored the circulation. Wee pink clouds of fresh blood furrowed here and there in spots up and town the toes.

Grunwalt looked up as he finished with the final toe. He looked into the man's face and he smiled a slow, cognitive smile. The man, too, began to smile benignly.

I think it will be all right now, said Grunwalt. I think it will be fine. You have a disjointed disporia tremens, said Grunwalt. Did you know that? Yes, said the tax man. Oh, yes.

Some Questions We, as We Are About to Buy in Lawn City, Ask Ourselves:

1. What do we know about the quality of life in Lawn City?
2. Can we send our children to the public schools?
3. Are we buying a way of life or are we simply purchasing property?
4. Can we find a six-room center-hall colonial on an attractive quarter-acre plot for under three quarters of a mil?
5. How do we go about volunteering for something or other?
6. Is Lawn City accessible by boat?

7. Can we sell our house within two years for at least sixty percent more than we pay today?
8. How often do they pick up the garbage?
9. Is it true that, in case of foreign attack, plans are ready for implementation which would require Lawn City residents to house and feed six million residents of the inner city?
10. Are liquor stores open weeknights? Sundays?
11. Do we get a sticker for the BMW that indicates, even when we are away from town, that we are Lawn City residents?
12. Are cabin cruisers included in the personal property tax even though they are moored in Larchmont?

Grunwalt and I, before moving to Lawn City, lived beside each other on Main Street in New Rochelle. We were upstairs from a janitorial supply store. He was on the other side of the hall in a congruent apartment to my own. His wife of the time looked very much like my own. He would have no children, so I, too, would have no children although now, as I look back, I wonder if I did the right thing. One can go overboard sometimes trying not to disturb other people's feelings.

In those days, Grunwalt was working down at Sears loading forty-five-foot trailer trucks by day and attending night school. His feet killed him, he always said in those days. This is why he got interested in podiatry. At night he would come over to my apartment and sit on a couch that was exactly like his own. They both faced tiny nine-inch Capehart television screens which were built into enormous fruitwood cabinets. We would suck a beer or two and discuss his newfound interest. Feet, I can remember him saying, are essential. Enormously important. We would miss them severely in their absence. If they were cut off in a train accident, then we would worry.

Grunwalt moved out and I lost track of him. Like many before him, he went out one night to get a pack of butts and never returned. His wife was heart-broken but I was told later that she had been visited by a premonition. Something like that had to happen, she said. A man doesn't go to night school for nothing, she said to me a week after his disappearance. He has thoughts of moving up and I don't fit in with his fancy friends at night school. He should die from a dog's teeth.

I had a refrigerator full of beer when he left, Ballantine cans which I had kept solely for him, for our nightly talks when he returned from Sears before he would walk down Main Street and up North Avenue with a stack of books under his arm. I'm not blaming on him the many years I spent as a hopeless alcoholic but there never would have been beer one in the house if he hadn't lived across the hall and I tell you this from my heart of hearts.

Years later, we ran into each other. A phalanx of relatives had died, leaving my wife and myself a tidy sum. We went house hunting and ended up driving around Lawn City, sitting in the back of a Chinese lady's cream-colored Seville. Here we were with this lady broker, walking up the front lawn of an expanded red ranch that needed work when I saw him next door in front of another expanded red ranch that needed work. He was pushing an expensive Toro grass trimmer with a leaf bag attached. He wore a pair of expensive tennis shorts and an Izod golf shirt, the kind with the little alligator sewn over the left tit.

Grunwalt, I hollered over the noise of the lawn mower. *Can it be you?*

He turned the machine down to a low growl and walked slowly toward me, my wife, the Chinese. He was squinting and I noticed deep lines had developed on his brow and there was a Howdy-Doody thing happening around his mouth. Two cavernous furrows divided the far corners of his lips from his always prominent and exceedingly round cheekbones.

My gardener has been taken ill were the first words he spoke to me in fourteen years. I'm having difficulty operating this machine. I hope we understand each other, he said. I don't clip my own grass.

Certainly not, I said. But I don't believe you recognize me. Remember the old apartment on top of the janitorial supply store? Remember the beers, the Sears Roebuck trucks?

No, he said. You've mistaken me for another. I am a podiatrist. A physician. He cast a quick glance at the Chinese lady, afraid his cover had been broken, his beard unhooked from his ear.

He told me later, in privacy, that he feared the Chinese. They carry stories, he said. It would be all over Lawn City in a matter of hours if she smelled a fish, if she divined that he had once worked at manual labor. These are not the days, nor is this the place, he said, for the self-made. People here expect a certain monetary and familial continuity. If one is not born here, one is expected to intern at Rye. Harvard née Choate. Don't tell them where you're from, he cautioned, unless you like to play it dangerously. You'll never enjoy a Scotch and water again in decent company. There will be no invitations. You will be drinking beer in your bedroom watching Merv Griffin.

He never once asked about his wife, which is just as

well. There is a thin line one does not cross. And too, it is a well-known fact that it is unproductive to rehash the past. You meet someone you haven't seen in fourteen years, he asks you what's new, and you very honestly just shrug your shoulders.

Gorbachev's Wife

Gorbachev's wife, man. Twenty, thirty little dudes, man, all wrapping swatchyards around her bod, man. They go dress this momma up, show the watchful eye of the world how a Russian lady can step out, too. Pretty soon, man, she be knockin the shit out of a Wilson official over the nets at Monaco. Daddy G be in the press box suckin on a Scotch sour, a Brunschwig and Fils jacket, white kicks and a Madras belt. We go see a movie tonight then do some Dom Perignon and I hope somebody show up who can tell a joke. Daddy G be tired of lookin cross two feet at George Shultz look like a basset hound with a thing on his mind.

Daydew Ron Ron, man. Say jes give to me a million million mile of forest properties with a big wide horse and let me ride to the range where the West commences, saddle up my ass till I lose my senses. Ron's wife, man. One of the true tiny women of the world, man. The little lady, man. She be shook so many hands her hand be shakin, waitin on the next shake-it-up. Hello, hello, hello. You look so *dear*, dear. Oh, you be the Queen Prince of Wakamolea. Didn't even know they had one there. Your people are *so* dignified. I read about that. Ron never stops talking if I could jes get him down off that golden palomino a gift from the King of Slam what a lovely family. Do you know them?

Princess Di, man. Her hair be doin something to *me*. Change the gown, bitch. She be big too, on a vertical run. Be eatin peas off the head of the Royal Crown Prince. The dude be one polo playing sonofabitch. Give to me a mallet, he say; let me ride this bay nag to the goal posts. Hand me up some brilliantine.

Got to get my dead ass on a horse say Daddy G. The peoples think I don't do sports. Buy me up a big size Jimmy Carter shirt and call a man for a hat.

Me, you and the Prince of Wales, say Ron. Let them have Bronson, Eastwood, and Sergio Leone. See who get knock down from the horse. What the fuck. Let the women go to the flower show.

Gorbachev's wife, man. Be runnin in the bars with Bianca J and Margaret T. Say let's go to Princeton see what Brooke Shields be dressed up in today while the boys have some playtime. We talk lady talk. He leave his underwear hangin up on the lampshades too? If the world only knowed.

Manila, man. Marcos's old lady, man. One thing, man. She will get it done like she said it: Get every one of the peoples where they can speak man, *clearly*. It's a goal, man. It's a start. Order up some dresses from the dress man, man. Put them on my old man's card. If Arafat come here, man, don't let him use the bathroom. Build up one of them *temporaries* and burn it down when he leave. I think that man be carrying more than a gun, man. Look like he might have a boil.

Marcos he work it on out with a Arabian stallion, man. So he be ready for to ride at the Summit. He wish to be at the hill for to have *his* two fucking cents.

Jaruzelski, man. How this man can come to the fashion show? This one monumental task, man, to dress this dude up. Charge the man some Foster Grants. Never, say Mrs. J—never did trust no old dude be havin medals all stuck up on his front coat day and night, look out at you with one-way shades on his eyeball. What those eyes *do* behind that shit? Mrs. J see him ride on off down the streets of Cracow whippin on the ass of a Budweiser beer horse. Roadwork for the Summit. I be there, say Ski-man. George C. Scott be play me in the movie of the times of my life.

Margaret Thatcher, man. Side-saddle Peg. Be ride to the hill with Ron Ron, Charlie heir-to-the-throne. Scarfs be blowin back to the breeze like the ghost of Isadora Duncan. Mr. Thatcher, man. Who *is* this dude? Where he be? Epsom Downs. Say give the two pound on the five horse. Say I'm getting harried in the mornin. Margaret having her hair done, she can't be answering fucking questions right now.

Jerry Ford, man. He want to go, too. Clumsy dude be keep havin mud on his kneebone of his Botany 500 from he fall down all over the first tee. Ho ho ho he say. Ho ho de ho ho. Think maybe to split the fee for the golf cart with Tricky Dick for to have advisory position at the Summit. What his number? Betty? We have him down on a pad?

Ted Kennedy, man. Ain't got no country yet, man. But got him some Kennedy teeth that will not quit. Keep them shined *up*. He will sail to the Summit. How about a island, he say to Tip O'Neill. How bout we do this thing on a island? *Somebody* must owe you a favor. How in hell, say the Speaker, can Mister President's horse get to a island with him up *on* it? Use your shitbrains head. Could I wear shorts? say T.K. Could I once? And bring a girl? Would the peoples frown on that shit? I will commence a poll. I might could get Ireland, say Tip. Might. If I could keep my mouth shut one, and two, yours.

Mubarak, man. Head like a water buffalo. Eight sheets to the turban, man. What if that ain't a bunch of sheet? He too be comin up over the hill sayin: Can Egypt get itself a word in edgewise with all you goddam motormouths? Can Egypt speak to the situation? Ron Ron say: I race you with my golden palomino the gift of the King of Slam, versus your long-neck camel for the Nile River. If you win, I will sign over to you Miami of Ohio. Deal?

Don't even *own* the Nile River say he, and if en I did, would I give it to *you*? Maybe you would enjoy another oil crisis? *That*, say Ron Ron, I can get some from Prince Charles's head when he let me play with it for a short time.

Gorbachev's wife, man. Ron Ron's wife, man. Ferraro, man. Princess Di, Brooke Astor, Brooke Shields, Billy Joel's wife, man. Diana Vreeling, Mamma Cass, man. Tina Turner, man. Lady Marchmain, man. Barbara Wa Wa, man. Molly Bloom, man. Alice Toklas, Phyllis George, man. Jackie Kennedy, Tricia Nixon and Mrs. Rambo Marine. George Hamilton's girlfriend, man. LuLu's back in town. Lotte Lenya, Mary Steenburgen, Robyn Smith, Gorgeous George's sister-in-law, June Taylor's Dancers, Sargent Shriver's kids, man. Meryl Streep, man. Ruby Dee and Sue Simmons. Thoroughly modern Millie. What a party, man. Cocktails on the first tee. Watch the old serious dudes ride out on the horseflesh. Ride out to get the world saved.

Whole lot of horses' asses be lookin at the ladies in the face. So what! It's the world got to be saved. Gorbachev's wife, man. That how it start. Dressed up like the Bride of Rockenstein. Didn't know she had the flair, man. Confess to a mutual thread to make it all possible. The height of dressedence. We will *film* this for prosperity. And don't them boys look cute mingled up on the first green astride them chargers! What is the first bitch of the peoples in your boundaries, we can hear one, loudest one say. What can we do as the top stave of humanity to alleviate the tensions your subjects verse? *What* can we do? What can we *do*?

Mayberry

He was a judge and he wore suspenders because he was an old-time judge. They all said once: "He'll be a judge someday," and he did. The years went by like that, snap, and he was a judge. They had a little town and they needed a new judge and naturally he was the one who would be it.

In times past, the first few things he judged were easy, like cakes and pies. "I judge this one," he would say, and he would point to the one he meant and that would be it, the judging would be over and he would have a drink.

"I enjoy drinking more than, say, golf," he answered the reporter who was assigned to write him up, write something on the judge for the papers. "I enjoy classical music and collecting ceramics," said the judge, "but like everyone else, some day I would like to have a family I could boss around. I would like to build a cabin outside of town and grow things, maybe start a theater group. Most people think judges are really only into judging, but we enjoy other things, things that most ordinary people do."

This was the article that catapulted him into prominence. This was the one that got him the job in Mayberry with Andy. Andy was the sheriff. Aunt Bea was the aunt. Barney was the undersheriff. And Opie was the kid.

The judge started drinking with Andy in the afternoons. Andy was supposed to pick up Opie from school at three o'clock, something he had been doing faithfully for two or three years, but now he was pretty well lit-up by that time and Opie would just sit on the steps for an hour or two and then start to walk. Sometimes he would get picked up by Floyd the barber or Howard the guy who worked as a clerk in the courthouse.

One night late in October when Aunt Bea reckoned she had been through enough of this, she finished the dishes, put Opie to bed, and asked Andy to sit down on the old paisley-pattern couch. She got him a cup of tea and started to shoot the questions at him real nice at first, because that was her style.

"Andy, something's been bothering you and I'd like to know what it is."

"Oh, I'm all right, Aunt Bea. I just like to have a little taste now and again. I'm tired of this damned khaki uniform and this silly pompadour. The judge thinks I might look better in a blazer and he suggests I should have my hair cut back on the top and let it grow out on the sides to cover my ears a little bit, and I think he's right."

"So, it's the judge." She sat down beside him and brushed at the part of the dress that covered her lap.

————————

The man filled the mug with J&B and set it again in front of the judge. "I might lock up the whole town," said he.

"One by one." He looked the bartender square in the eyes, searching for the slightest nuance of disapprobation. The judge was spare of form and height, but not fragile.

Opie was sick of walking home from school because in real life he was a lazy kid. He stuffed himself with Mounds bars day and night and he brushed his teeth only when the mood ran him down. He had been sucking Marlboro Lights behind the gym since the second semester of last year and in his red/yellow 'fro, he wore a violet comb-pik, the handle of which stuck straight up into the air. Once, a startled Aunt Bea had caught him going through her jewelry box looking for a lobe ring.

―――――――

"Why can't you stay home and drink with me, Andy?" asked Aunt Bea. "We could have a nice little Amaretto shooter now and again. Or a Crème de Cacao. And no one would be the wiser."

"It's not the same," said Andy. "Oh, I know how you feel, but a man has to go out and tie on a load by hisself every day or two. It's part of manhood. And the judge says there's a job might open up in Mount Pilot where it's more professional-like. Everybody knows one's business hereabouts. There's even some talk about cutting out my gasoline allowance because they say I'm gallivanting around in the old Ford on personal business. What kind of personal business could I have? And what kind of way is that to talk about your own sheriff?"

"Oh that Mrs. Jessups! I knew it."

"Well, it's not just Mrs. Jessups, Aunt Bea. It's Clara and it's Goober and the mayor, and, if you must know, I think Barney's right there in the thick of it. He'd loooooove to see my big ass brought up on charges so's he could be the kingfish hereabouts."

"Oh, Andy!"

———————

After that conversation, Andy and the judge proceeded to drink together for eight or twelve years running. The job never did open up in Mount Pilot, and the judge said the hell *with* it. He began to finish up early at about ten-thirty in the mornings and he would send a car around for Andy at the jailroom. Sometimes they would have coffee first at the Chat and Chew, but usually they would go right to the bar. Most times they would run into Otis Campbell. Otis was the kind of a drunk the judge didn't really like to get plowed with because Otis was a known misdemeanant and he had no dignity or position in his real life. The judge liked to keep a little fashionability in his facings but one day OC turned him on to a splendid rum cooler julep and they drew a little closer.

"That boy of yours never seems to get any age on him," said the judge to Andy one afternoon. "He's a perpetual child. Maybe he should grow him a moustache, make him look taller or something. We'll get him a job in the court-house. That guy Howard's got to go anyways. He's got a voice like a flute that's been bent all out of shape. Time to send him packing."

"He's a weasel," said Andy. "He's spreading innuendoes about me and Aunt Bea. Howard, I mean."

"I'll draw up some papers, have him locked up," said the judge. "Open up the spot for the kid. What kind of name is that, *Opie*, anyways?" asked the judge.

"French," said Andy. "I named him after the inventor of the atom bomb."

———————

Andy and Otis got to where they could tell you the names of the different composers and the symphonies because the judge always had a transistor radio attached to his belt and tuned in to a classical station. One night in December, Andy made up this drink from the bottles he had in his car and called it a Gin Night-Crawler, and the three of them sat in the back of the squad car parked at a pump at Goober's station and they sang the complete *Messiah* as best they could. Then they fell asleep and like to froze to death before Barney spotted them there and drove Andy's car inside one of the bays where it was warm enough for a body to survive the night.

"We should go to Europe sometime," said the judge. "The three of us. I'd like to hear some music in person and see the marble statues and the gondola-men. Only thing, they'd have to be a restaurant nearby. With a ice machine. I hate to death them room-temperature cocktails."

———————

Goober and Helen started to go to the cinema together on Saturdays, doubling with Barney and Thelma-Lou. "I never knew she'd stoop that low," said Andy. "I don't mean anything bad about Goober, but that's *crazy*. Imagine if I had died. She'd be going around with Goober the gas-station guy. I guess I held myself up too high."

"You can never have too much humility," said Otis.

"Be a cynic," said the judge, "and you're never disappointed. I'd burn the filling station down were it me. See how she likes *that*."

"He bought hisself a condo," said Otis. "On top of the newspaper office. Helen's giving him voice lessons for to get the job on 'Monday Night Football' to tell about what's going on. I could see where a woman could fall for *him*. He's re-versed his life a hundred and eighty turnaround. When he sings he gots a voice like a meadowlark."

"You got him confused with that other geek guy, Gomer," said Andy. "This here's Goober. Gomer's that marine guy. Goober would kill him in a fight. He'd *wrench* him to death. Goober's a greasy guy. He wouldn't care about getting dirty whereas Gomer always impressed me as being sort of a sissy."

"I like Goober," said the judge. "He always gives me one of those little cardboard Christmas tree things to hang from my rearview mirror to kill the smell."

"He's a lovely boy," said Otis. "I had him confused for a slight moment but now I know the boy."

"Him and Helen," said Andy. "Ain't that enough to throw you for a loop."

———————

Aunt Bea had no one home so she had to start taking Opie with her to the Geraldine Ferraro '88 meetings. They were held at Sue Bell Foster's house because Sue Belle had been the one who had put up Harry Truman's advance man's niece when they swung through town that time. Sue Belle had spoke it up from way back saying we needed a woman at the top. Aunt Bea wasn't too sure if we needed a woman at the *top*. What she *did* know was *she* needed to get out of the house now and again to keep a grip on her sanity. She hoped Opie's being around all those women would not make him start talking like poor Truman Capote. But if it were that or stay home, it would be *that* as far as she was concerned.

Coming back from the Ferraro folderol, Aunt Bea and Opie found Andy sleeping on the front lawn. It was after ten at night and at first, from a distance, Aunt Bea thought someone had left the wheelbarrow out, but as they came closer, she saw what appeared to be a human form and she recognized Andy's new blue blazer and his old wrinkled khaki pants. The moon shards reflecting off the old ironed-shiny pants played for a moment a little ning-light game with her eyes.

For one long moment, she felt very small, almost minuscule, and Andy was a white-man mountain range that she would somehow, with Opie, have to circumambulate. His enormous ossified bulk had long figuratively lain between her and her happy home. Now a new, literal meaning had taken form. Things that at one time had endeared him to her—the enormous ears, the strange teeth that seemed to shove and elbow one another aside like little enameled women at the door of a fire sale—began now to curdle her colon. She went around him, pushing the boy ahead with a lefthanded grip on his arm and holding her right palm over his eyes.

"That looked like Pa," said Opie, now blinded to the horror of the scene by her palm, and lurching in the direction of Aunt Bea's insistence. "Was that Pa?"

"Oh, Opie," said Bea. "How can you think something as awful as that? Some drunken gentleman must have lost his way and stumbled into our yard. He'll go away soon enough. You slip on in now and get into your jammies and brush those teeth. When you're all done, Aunt Bea will make you a nice hot cocoa before you go to bed."

The following evening, Andy decided to take the night shift at the office to try to get his bolts torqued down. He had felt truly humiliated when he awoke that morning, eyeballs to the earth, and except for two inexpertly made Bloody Marys slugged down by dawnlight at the kitchen sink and a gin screwdriver sipped in the early afternoon, he had wandered through an entirely spiritless day.

When he pulled up at the office in the black and white, it was early evening. He noticed the blinds rustle at the big window in front, and he sat for a moment behind the wheel watching Barney's baby blues run slat to slat like a ferret in a froghollow.

"Hi, Ange," said Barney as Andy entered.

"Hey, what it is, Barn?" Andy greeted.

"Ange, the judge's been calling all day for you. Sounds worried sick. Says he called Aunt Bea and she tole him you had left town. Said he was afraid you fell in a ditch someplace."

"Now, what would I be doing in a ditch?"

"It wasn't me said it, Ange."

"Well, I'm sorry, Barn, but that's a right strange thing for a person to say—'in a ditch'—I don't *do* ditches. I would think that *you* would know that, of all people."

"Well, it's more serious than that, Ange. The judge dropped his drawers at the town meeting. Hung a moon on the whole bunch of them. Floyd's started a motion to have him impeached. Howard says he hasn't judged nothing right since he did that pie that one time."

Andy stuck his two hands in his pockets and he walked to the window. "That just sounds like plum, flat-out jealousy, Barn."

"Maybe so, Ange, but there's more than that. The judge threatened to lock up the whole town council. That's why he's been calling up. He wrote up some kind of a writ. I told him I couldn't do a thing until I talked to you. Ange, I'm scared. I know he's your friend, but that man's a nuclear weapon with the pin missing."

"If you keep talking like that, Barney, I might have to relieve you of command and bring in Goober like I did when you went on vacation to Mount Pilot."

"Andy, you wouldn't take my tin?"

"I'm not saying I would, Barn. But you got to envision the chain-of-command. This here's serious stuff. A judge can do whatever it is he wants to do. You have got to remember that you're just a wee-wee in the woods. You could be left out there by the side of the road just to be sniffed at."

Andy walked to the small mirror that hung up top behind the old green file cabinet. He ducked a little at the knees so the top of his head joined the picture, and he primped with his hands at the sides of his hair. "No sense both of us hanging out together here," he said. "I think I'll take a little spin around town, see what's what."

———————

The evening was full topped of Mayberry now. Lights were on in most of the open-late stores but Andy noticed that the streets seemed unusual quiet. Never was a whole lot of noise this time of day but when you're a sheriff for a stretch of distance, your ears start to pick up on certain silences as a perpetrator in its own self. Like if you have a bunch of small-fries in the house and you go ten or fifteen minutes without a holler fight or a crash, you know something terrible is in the planning stages.

Andy was smart enough to know that he was in bad need of some advice. What would Matt Dillon from the TV had did, pinned to the paneling in a situation like this? Answer: 1. Talk to Doc, maybe the last man in town with an elevator that went to the top. 2. Head on out on a journey around the state trying to find a circuit judge with a proper sheepskin who could give him an Ivy-League ruling on the matter. 3. Stop in at Miss Kitty's and get fried.

He rolled the black and white real slow down the main lane. He noticed up ahead the lights blazing from Floyd's shop window, and, as he slowed down to a snail crawl, he could see clearly that the place was jammed up with people. At first he thought there was a run on haircuts, but he quickly discarded that assumption as ludicrous. There was a meeting going on. And it no doubt had to do with *him*. And the judge.

A man he didn't recognize who was dressed all in black and looked like an aged Palladin watched him from inside and pointed to the car. Suddenly people turned, a few at a time, to face him in the street and then all of them, dozens, crowded to the window. Their eyes were opened wide and their mouths folded and unfolded like fish in a tank. Andy gunned the motor. The tires squealed. The car's rear end spun-out and for a moment he was sideways, caterwauling and heading directly for a storefront window across the street. Somehow, without taking his right foot off the floorboard, he got the old Ford under control, and, as though propelled by a slingshot, he roared away from the scene leaving behind him a horrid excretion of blue-black Wolf's Head haze.

Andy parked the vehicle outside of town and proceeded back on foot, careful when he got to the inskirts to stay to the alleys and the side roads. he utilized the time spent to ponder in depths his situation:

Aunt Bea was putting on weight and if their last few

conversations had meant anything, she was ready to vote *in* the Equal Rights Amendment and get herself a job as the check-out in Woolworth's, which could give her the opportunity to be rude to a dozen or so people a day, a luxury that she had previously believed, as with all women who were getting some age on them, had passed her by.

Opie was getting spacey on him, failing most of his subjects and saving up to buy an amplifier so he could irritate a wider range of people, a whole new audience up and down the street with the electric guitar he had bought for next to nothing from a coke addict in his class.

Goober was flitting around town all dressed up like Peter O'Toole trying to bogart his way into the gap that had been driven by fate between himself and Helen.

Floyd, the airhead he had befriended as an equal, was now organizing a lynch committee to see to it that he was properly ruined.

———

The judge was sitting with Otis at the bar when Andy arrived. Andy entered stealthily, like a house-breaker, and he looked slowly and carefully to either side as he approached the hardwood. The place was empty, as usual, except for them and the bartender.

"I guess you heard," said the judge.

"I guess I did," said Andy, with a sort of indignation, like it was the judge brought down all these troubles on his head.

"They brought in a hired gun," said the judge. "Black suit, silver-buckle things on his hat, business cards, face like a cactus melon."

"I seed him," said Andy. "What a horrible face."

"He don't worry me," said the judge. "I'll slap him with

so many statutes he'll think he's surrounded by paper mills."

"That's easy for you," said Andy. "But I'm the one has to get physical. I'm the executive branch."

"Don't get daffodil on me, A.T. When the going gets tough, the tough get going. This is Vince Lombardi territory. Fourth and one. Late in the game. No time-outs. We going to push it across. You and me. And Otis. Have a drink."

"I'll have a Brandy Alexander," said Andy to the bartender.

The judge cut him short. "Don't pull that candy-ass shit with me," he said. "Have a double J.W. Dant in a water glass and get aholt of yourself. We don't kick no pretty field goals. We gonna *run* it in." He motioned to the bartender and pointed to the bourbon bottle.

"We got ourselves some *UN*-happy campers out there," said Andy.

"If we can get through this one," said Otis, "if we can tough this one out, we got ten, twelve years of smooth sailing in front of us."

"Squirrel-off," said Andy. "You ain't nothin' but an extra suitcase. I need crap from you, I'll squeeze your head."

"The tension has got *to* him," said Otis to the judge.

"It's getting *ugly* out there," said Andy.

"Good times are never as good as they seem or bad times as bad," said the judge. "You learn that from recollection. That's why I'm the judge—I see things like that in the back of my mind."

Andy gulped his J.W. Dant.

"I may aspire to higher office," said the judge. "But you have my word right here and now that I won't test the waters until I clear up this thing right down to the small print."

"Sometimes I think I'd like to go back to the old Andy," said Andy.

"Can't," said the judge. "Them days is over. It can't *never* be the same as *that*. They ain't writin' shit like that no more."

Post Cards

LABRADOR

Don't talk to me you're chilly. It's cold up here, Jack. Take a leak in the woods you'll get an idea. Lumber is what makes us famous. Own a pair of boots that won't shut up. We're descended from Eskimos and we play whale games. You go to the zoo to see sea lions and penguins. You should have to live with these filthy creatures. Icebergs float by my door like taxicabs. My favorite TV show is "Bonanza." I'd like to see dust.

China, Right?

China man. Cholly, Cholly, Cholly. China man do rice, baby. Egg Foo Young. Dig on a rice paddy, you want to know what trouble is. My implements are old, man. Prehistoric. Balsa. My nights are like a wild dream. That's what it like in China. Want to talk to a fucking yak all night and into the next day? Dude keep asking you to loosen the yoke. Tries to make a friend of you. Why don't we talk, he say. Loosen the yoke. Leave it over there in the corner of the lean-to. Hang it on the yak knob. This way we can talk, get to know each other. Bullshit! Don't buy it. All you see is one big fat yak ass heading out over the flooded paddies. What do you know from this kind of trouble out there in Cleveland?

China man have every reason to believe hostility will rear its ugly head.

ST. CROIX

You can O.D. on a rum cooler, you don't dig yourself. The mens beat on old pots for a living and you swaggle blue gin from a hurricane lamp. God gave out trees here that won't quit. Sand is khaki sugar and Dior did the water. The fish look healthy, man. I mean they can *see* what they're eating. Everybody want to know what *De*troit is like. The cruise ship drops off the E.T.s, man. Knobby-kneed, hard-to-look-at gang of dudes. Everybody wants his fortune did.

Mamaroneck, N.Y.

Where the salt water meets the fresh. It's an Indian word. I'm in a bed-and-breakfast by the Sound. Old Victo. The rooms are slanted like the news. Go to the parlor, you need a tie to watch the Yankees. You can die here, they do the whole thing downstairs between innings. Bette Davis smokes in the attic. Every morning you pass the rolls around. Nothin' shakin but the leaves on the trees.

GREECE

Philosophy make it fun. Olympic gas, man. The rotor. The thing that goes in the water. When you got being and nothingness, we opt for the former, baby. That's *today* talking. Gulfs happened here. Each sea has a thousand arms. We did one golden age. You probably didn't have one of those. Don't worry about it. This is an old goddam country. We give out Revivals, Festivals, Fire, Drama, Vases, Myth, Gammas, Lambdas, etc., etc. Get the word out there. And Parthenon. Corfu?

Florida

It stay steady hot. Except they want to raise the price of oranges, then they do a frost. The Mouse live here. You can play with his ears, you pay the man. People like to do the beach. You find sand in your shorts *all* the time. Got a whale show all up and down the coast. You could buy a plastic belt. They going to send the Mouse on a rocket. It's for the childrens. He will drop mouse hats on Russia for to cheer up the grouchy mommalommas. That's the kind of place *this* is.

Sausalito

Sound like a sausage sack. Small sausage in a sack. Or a
gravy slop. It's not. It's where I am. It's where I send my
greeting from. Can you dig Mill Valley? Nearby, man.
Walkable! Can a youth find love at a night game? San
Francisco, baby. Not far. Not too far to go. Love in the
glove. Stealing's O.K., man. You get a raise. That's the
way it come down. I send you all my love from this small
sack sausage. That leave me empty, man.

Worrying

The other night I tried to put my head in a microwave oven and end it all. I mean this. If my regular oven were not broken down, I would have done the job, nice and simple. But my head wouldn't fit all the way in, even after I took out the rack and the grease pan. The top of my head became super-hot and uncomfortable so I said the hell with it and I opened up a bottle of Old St. Croix.

Hell of a move for an educated person, right? How could an English teacher with a rent-controlled apartment, a person who owes only thirty, forty dollars total overdue on the MasterCard put his head in a portable oven and push the broil button?

Easy. For one thing, having sort of a heightened sensitivity is a genuine burden. I mean you worry about things—things other people don't even consider. Like when the President talks about the Consumer Price Index, I worry. I worry about another gas crisis and the environment. I am a Friend of the Bronx Zoo and the Audubon Society because I worry about the animals. This kind of worrying costs cold, hard cash. This is not gratuitous worrying.

Lately, I am worried about the state of education in this country. I worry about these third-year kids in the college where I teach who can't read. These would be the village idiots of a past century and now they're juniors in college. Christ! It's hard to believe.

I assigned a two-page paper in September that was due on November fifteenth and I have four papers to correct. *Four.* This is out of twenty-seven students. About fifteen have had a death in the family. Two others play on the basketball team so they have trouble getting it together. One black kid, who might be my best student, told me he doesn't believe in writing papers for somebody because it perpetuates a slave/master mentality. He thinks we should discuss only "alternate points of view." Some of these kids think they're smart and I have to agree that there is a certain mental dexterity prerequisite to the avoidance of work without suffering the consequences.

"Don't fail any of these kids," says my boss, Wherling, who is head of the department. "These kids represent the future and we can't afford to discourage them. They'll come around," he says. "Give them a chance."

I've told him a dozen times that I think the whole thing is a disgrace, but each time he puts his index finger to his lips while I am in mid-sentence. "You would rather drive a truck?" he asks. "We have few enough English majors as it is. There will be no jobs for us. Do you follow me? If you fail them, they will lose interest."

"But I worry about these kids," I tell him. "I worry that they're wasting their time." Sometimes I wonder if he really knows how much I worry about these kids.

One day I am talking to the class about "The Waste Land." I am trying to get across the concept of death and regeneration taken together, like drowning in a spiritual sense and the baptism of rebirth. "Some treat death euphemistically in our culture," I tell them. "Others feel we should accept and attempt to transcend it. Death in one sense is a positive, a contribution to the future. Regeneration. This may be the irony inherent in all great poetry—that the waste land of our existence can be made fertile by suffering—by those who sacrifice themselves—greater love has no man and all that." There is a question from the back of the room: "What are all those burnt-out frizzles on your head? You put your head in a microwave oven?

Wherling has introduced a number of new courses for the spring semester: *An Introduction to Bob Dylan*; *Hallucinogens and Poetry*; *Muhammad Ali: Poet or Charlatan*; *The Large Fish in Literature: Moby Dick Through Jaws*; and *The Literature of Explicit Sex*.

"I'm worried about your choice of new courses," I tell him. "For one thing, Moby Dick wasn't a fish. Jaws may be a fish, that I couldn't tell you, but Moby Dick was *not* a fish. We might be doing our students a disservice."

"Classes," he says, "are already filled." He is probing one of his colossal nasal orifices with his index finger. "I hate to say this," says he, "but you appear to be losing your touch. How old are you anyway? Thirty-four? Stay out of the sun. Your hair is frizzling up. It makes you look aged."

"I'm thinking of changing occupations," I tell him. "Could you advise me?"

"You're not thinking of leaving teaching?"

"I don't know," I say honestly. "I just wonder where I fit in anymore."

"There's room for you here," he says. "Still there are certain courses which we are almost mandated to offer. Nobody wants to teach John Donne anymore, or *any* of the Metaphysicals for that matter. And the Victorians. Most of the faculty, I'm afraid, is of the opinion that all of them are irrevelant."

"Surely," I say, "you mean irrelevant."

"What I mean *is* that there are some former heavy-hitters of literature who have fallen into disfavor, as it were. Not to say that I agree, if you know what I mean."

"I'm not much of a scholar," I admit to him, "but I will do what I can." I worry about people who think John Donne is irrelevant.

"Don't you ever worry about anything?" asks my father. "You just float through life. A month off at Christmas, all the holidays, Easter recess, holy days of obligation, Passover, lunchtime every day. You never miss. It's all charted out for you. I haven't had a day off in forty years and you teach twelve miserable hours a week for a few weeks at a time. You don't have a worry in the world. What kind of way is that to live?"

"I worry about my students. I worry about my twelve-year-old Volvo. I worry about you, Pop."

"You worry about *me*? Don't worry about *me*. I handle *my* life. A Ph.D. today is worth a high school equivalency in the forties. Your brother Norman's on the cops. Makes his money. He's got his feet on the ground. Five kids and they're all eating."

And I worry about Norman. My brother Norman.

Someday I'll teach his kids. I worry about having to explain to him that they'll all fail if they don't do the work.

Today I told my class how worried I was that they were all going to fail. I have received four papers, I said, four out of twenty-seven. And those four are so poorly thought-out and wretchedly written that I can't give any one of them a passing grade. Someone has to take a stand, I said. A bankruptcy is giving birth here and someone has to take responsibility.

"You can't be as bad as all that. Every one of you has been sitting in a classroom five hours a day five days a week for the past fourteen years. My God! And no one here can compose a compound sentence or punctuate a friendly letter. Where are we going? Is it over? Has it ended? Sometimes I feel like putting my head in an oven."

As the bell rang and I was putting my books into my valise, someone in the pushing crowd by the door muttered in a horrible, guttural tone, "Yeah, stick your head in the oven, you meatball." I didn't even turn or look up. You tell me, what would be the point?

Wherling is sitting at the far end of the faculty lounge with a few of his hangers-on from the English faculty. They are all laughing uproariously at one of his simple-ass jokes when I hit him on the head with a very nice edition of *W. H. Auden's Complete Poems* that was a gift to me from a girl I used to know. I acted impulsively. Had I more time to think, I would have used the Norton Anthology which is much heavier and carries less sentimental value.

He is looking at me quizzically. His mouth is hanging open and one arm of his glasses hangs down over his myronic nose. Everyone is very quiet for a change, and then

Wherling comes out with a real gem:

"Have you lost your mind?" he asks. "Your job has wings, *friend*. Your *tenure* is swinging in the wind," he says, gesticulating with the very same dirty digit with which he excavates his nostrils.

"I am going to blow up this entire room and apply for the Nobel Peace Prize," I tell him. They are staring at my valise. "I'm worried about all of you," I say. "I'm worried. The other night I tried to kill myself. Does any one of you know what that means?"

Someone grabs me from behind and before I know what's happening, they have me pinned to the wall and some guy from Speech is going through my briefcase.

"A Norton Anthology, *A Happy Death* by Camus, some Jane Austen, a Charlotte Brontë novel," says the Speech guy. "Nothing explosive here."

"You're finished," screams Wherling. "You're done. Severed. Out. Terminated."

"How could you do it?" asks Mary Brady, a Sociology instructor.

"I was worried," I say. "I worry."

"But you've made a spectacle of yourself. You're out of a job. You may never work *again*."

"That's not my problem," I tell her. "You can't worry about everything. You can't worry about every little goddamned thing."

Sleepy Hollow

Was when we to the graveyard went, checked out the stones. Walked high down the grass, climbed two hills, flagled wood, strendled a stream strembling through. An old Dutch Craven. Place of simple, stergend people, unhurried in their verdin lives, grackel and God-fearing, grain fed and willow shaded sand stone slabs.

Once a year, in the fall when the slides of the Hudson stinge to the eye from red red to the high down drift brown. It's Tarrytown. The bridge of wide plank Brom Bones straddles Pocantico on the river top where Ichabod Crane came barrelassing by on Old Gunpowder long kneebone whipping that light nag to the Tappan Zee. That's fear, man. That's eyeballs to the black nothing.

There, feelbe down the sloping through soft earth hollow. Old years have gained this sleep and wish them well. Across the road, George Washington rest brown gravy on his grits, got the troops grazled and sturdy for battle, foggled down flagons of warm rum groggles and banged with his pointing finger on a woodgrain tooth thinking of a wrinkle for muscooting the cannons and manueling his arms. History, man. All what we be.

So once a year, here, in the tenth month the valley and hill do produce one winter son. Coloren bright like the inner eye of a god's fashion lunch. Modeling oak and chestnut whip through the breeze. Wear wool for the infant hawk and swaddle his scarf to the neck, loan him some shades. Pumpkins try to show up. Hollow bones are in the wings. This hawk could be father to the man.

Farther up, the hill can judge the Hudson. Real lives once cut in fieldstone say: Work this land. That wife, some faithful children straight and good enough for him, for me. All fear the witch, and so I do. Quiet times are what we're owed. Men alive are trouble. Makers.

A Life
for the Theater

Richie Guarini and Richie Flynn. R for Richie and D for Flynn because D stands for Dick, another way to say Richie. You can't have two Richies, said R, like you can't have Richie and Richie or R and R. So how about Richie and Dick, or R and D for short? R and R would sound too much like rest and recreation or recuperation. And G and F sort of sounds like a deli. How about R and D?

Who gives a royal shit, said D.

This way, said R, if something breaks down or something when we tow it, nobody knows who the fuck is who. Get it?

R was the brains, the motivation. In '84 he worked in a Hess station and saw it come and go. He knew the flow. He recognized the need. D carried a torch for a little honey in Portchester and liked to blow dope. R considered this, but who wants to run a tow-truck company alone? You never see it. And R and D sounded important, like the Mafia. Nobody would play games with a company called R and D Towing. Even the Mafia would have to make a call to see if this outfit was connected. R sensed, correctly, that they could hand somebody a bill and somebody would pay it. People don't like to live dangerously. That much he knew.

So they bought an old Gimmy tow truck and R painted it black with a brush and lettered it with an R letter in gold from Librett's Hardware and a D letter. D went to the beach. D goes: I'm no good at painting and that shit; I'd only screw it up. So let me know over the weekend what's what and when we start to tow the asses off these people.

The next Monday R drove the truck and D sat shotgun and smoked a few bones and drank a Diet Pepsi. R made him throw the roaches out the window so they wouldn't end up in the ashtray. They looked all day for somebody to tow into a body shop or a service station. When the sun sank they decided to have a few beers.

We need a direction, said R, finally. Today I get the feeling we're shoveling shit against the tide, you know what I mean? He was drinking now and when he drank, he cursed a lot more than usual and he smoked True 100s.

There's too many tow-truck companies out there, said D. We hit saturation. Maybe in some other part of the country, but not here. We're too close to the Big Apple.

Shit, said R. He ordered a beer. We can't do this for the rest of our lives.

Driving around like two shitforbrains, said D. We don't even know if this thing works—the lift.

Didn't he show you? asked R. I thought the guy showed

you while I was taking a leak. I came back, you said everything is O.K.

Shit, he showed me the levers and stuff and made the back thing go up, but there weren't no car attached. How do we even know the fucker works?

R ordered two more beers and D played the juke box. When he came back to his chair, R said to him: This is incredible. What if we have to hook up a car, how do we do it?

You're the one who went and took a leak, said D. At least I stood there with this thing.

But why didn't you ask him?

Why didn't you?

I was takin' a leak, or chrissakes. I figured you could show me later, when we hooked up the first shitbox.

D took a long swallow of the Bass Ale. He put down the bottle. I didn't want to make the guy figure we didn't know all this stuff. You were in the Hess station eight months.

We didn't do no repairs, said R. We just pumped the piss in the tanks.

What a fuckin' let-down, said D. He was thinking maybe he would join the air force and be a jet mechanic.

R dropped D off where he lived with his parents and then took another swing downtown in case there might be an accident.

Tuesday D took the truck alone and he held up the Shopwell store on Pelham Road. He brought a shotgun in with him stuck up under an old ankle-length army coat. He shoved it up under a fat lady's nose on aisle six which was closest to the door. The papers didn't say how much he got but somebody saw R and D on the tow-truck door and a little while later the cops showed up at R's house while his old man was watering the lawn.

Is this the home of R, they asked, of R and D Towing? The old man already had the charcoals going on the grill. We're having corn on the cob and chiliburgers, said the old man. You boys are welcome if you're so inclined. The old man was a volunteer fireman and he knew what it was like to get hungry while you're on the job.

We'll sit a spell, said the taller policeman of the two. How long before you throw this shit on the grill?

The coals were starting to get white. The old man checked the grill and glanced at the little portable table to see how many corns he had and would the chili go far enough. I'll throw it on now, he said.

We'll have to speak to R sooner or later, said the shorter policeman, but right now I could use one of them cold greenies. The old man had a small Rubbermaid garbage can full of ice and Heinekens which he had planned would mellow him off into the evening. He extracted two which were packed in upside down and cold as hell.

Don't open mine, said the tall policeman. I'd like to hold it here in my hands and cool down my palms. I had to shoot at a man about ten this morning.

R's old man put one greenie on the table in front of the tall policeman, popped the top on the other Heinie and handed it to the short, heavy-set policeman.

'Preciate it, said the shorty. He took a long swig on the bottle neck and removed his hat and poured the rest over his head. What's the humidity index? he asked. Must be a hundred eighty-frieken-five. Holy shit! Pop me another of them green suckers, he said.

R isn't tryin' to get away or nothin', is he, asked the tall policeman. I don't want to have to shoot him in a residential neighborhood.

You can't expend two bullets on the same day on separate calls, said the short, fat policeman. They'll be havin' us fill out forms into next week. *I'll* shoot him if he's got to be shot. They'd be all over you like they done to Nixon. He slapped five meaningfully with the tall policeman.

The corn, wrapped up in tin foil with butter inside was starting to smoke so the old man rolled them off the grill with a ladle and let them fall on the table.

I wonder, said the tall policeman, what would make a kid from a nice neighborhood do something like that with the Shopwell market?

Kids, I guess, said the old man. It's different today.

My kid's a junior at Hofstra, said the littler policeman. Normal things—wrecked the Ford wagon, like that. If I caught him with a gun, I'd shove it up his ass.

I should have done more of that, said the old man. These kids today live the life of Riley.

Not my kid, said the small policeman. I'd kick his butt from East St. Louis to the river. John here never had no kids. He's got no idea. You buy a house and raise a kid in it and ten years later you throw the house away. It's shot. The rugs are wore, the toilet don't work, the sheetrock is all cracked from the rock and roll music. The stairs get rotted that lead up to the porch and even the porch starts to lean. They play those jumping games.

I know, said the old man. I've tried to keep up with it. I'm all the time nailing something back or fixing cabinets that sprung or cementing in flagstones that heaved.

You wouldn't have that if you didn't have kids, said the short policeman. You wouldn't have none of it. You'd just set back and watch the property appreciate.

Upstairs, R was sitting in his room listening to a Tony Bennett. That morning he had received a note in the mailbox. D said he was going to Bar Harbor, Maine, and he had done something bad and if the police came, would R take the rap just this once and D would make it up to him. R didn't like the sound of it. He knew in the prisons when they played any tunes at all it was all disco and Motown stuff. That's one thing you could say about a rough crowd—they were into the kind of music that meant nothing to him. He couldn't picture himself sharpening spoons for fights in the dark tunnels that connected the prison buildings. On the other hand, how could he leave his partner hanging in a situation like this? If D went to prison, D had little chance of getting rehabilitated, only get worse. R felt he himself might be able to do a little easy time if he had a couple months to get himself in shape. Then, when he got out, he could move up to Bar Harbor where D would have had the time to get the towing thing built up and D would take him in like in the Jimmy Cagney movies. But then again, he would just as soon not go to jail at all, just hang around the house until something else came up.

The old man and the policemen ate the corns and threw the cobs over by the hedge.

If I had it to do over, I'd never be an officer, said the small policeman. It gets to grate on you. It just *grates* on you. It's only two years since they put air-conditioning in the sector cars. When it happened, I thought it would change my life. Wanna know what? It's the same shit, hot or cold.

I wanted R to take the test for the cops, said the old man. But he wouldn't.

Probably looks down on police officers, said the tall cop. That's the way some kids are. They think walking around with dirty underwear and a crummy T-shirt is the end-all. There's more to life than that.

172

I'm still trying to get him to take the next test, said the old man. I told him, you get a pension, vacations, personal days. And you don't have to do nothin' but ride around all day.

It won't be so easy for him now, with a felony on his record, said the tall policeman. They're getting stricter on that, unless you know somebody.

I think I'll kick his ass just for drill, said the short policeman. I hate these smart-ass kids who don't like cops. He'll like cops when *I* get through with him.

He needs a good beating, said the old man. I've been neglect on that.

You got any more beer? asked the short policeman.

I'll do one, too, said the other officer. Might as well get shit-faced here as someplace else.

This was a good town, said the short policeman, until the niggers started coming in. He struggled from his chair to his feet and walked a few yards to the hedge. He looked over to the yard next door. Any niggers next door here?

No, said the old man. This is middle-class here. Upper-middle. Not rich. Sort of upper.

The policeman turned from the hedge and faced the old man. We got niggers now livin' right next to police headquarters. Right next door! You walk out of police headquarters, you see a nigger first thing. Purple shirts and shit. Hats. Shit like that.

Never woulda believed to see that twenty, thirty years ago, said the old man.

We had one nigger in the whole class at high school, said the short policeman. One shine out of, I don't know, two, three thousand. We kicked *his* ass good every now and again.

Have to, said the old man.

He comes in one day with a red beret on his head. We kicked his ass real good. Eight, ten of us to one. That's the way it used to be.

No more, said the tall policeman.

No, shit no, said the short policeman.

Today they put the nigger on a pedestal.

And the kids follow in their footsteps, said the tall policeman. They walk and talk like the niggers do. Dirty, filthy fucking mouths.

That's where your kid got it from, said the short policeman to the old man. Hangin' out with niggers. I guarantee it. We have to lock him up. I almost forgot. I feel sorry for him. They'll throw him in a cell with a shitload of niggers.

He asked for it, said the tall policeman. Was it my kid, I'd kick his ass so bad he'd think he was surrounded by six ass-kicking machines. They could throw *me* in jail afterwards, I wouldn't give a shit.

He's a good boy, said the father. He must of got in, like you say, with some niggers. These kids, they leave the house for a few hours, you don't know where they go.

Too late for that now, said the short policeman. Now his ass is in the sling.

He started hanging around with D, said the old man. I don't know how I let it go on. They were gonna buy a tow truck. I don't know how I didn't see it coming.

Two flat tires, said the short policeman. Two numb-nutses.

They started rolling their own cigarettes, said the old man. I told them to do Marlboros but they wouldn't listen to me.

Now we have the right to search the house, said the tall policeman, after what you said.

They'd never bring it into *my* house, said the old man. They know better than that.

Probably stashed it in the garage, said the short policeman. They put it out of the way, like so you don't stumble on it. That's the M.O. We had a garage fire on Ellenton Avenue this spring, all the firefighters got high on the smoke. They was dancin' in the street sprayin' water hoses on each other 'til the Chief got there. *He* brought it to a screetchin' halt.

We'll have to toss the garage too, said the tall policeman. Say, you got any Canadian whiskey?

Sure, said the old man. Why don't we go inside. I'll mix some drinks and I'll introduce you to R.

I'd like to *meet* that boy, said the short policeman. I'd like to hurry up and put my size twelve where the sun don't shine.

ACT I
SCENE II
EVERYBODY GOES INSIDE

Living room has stairs going up stage left.

The two policemen lounge on large chairs at either end of the room. The old man sits nervously in a straight chair in the middle of the two who are somewhat distanced from one another. Each policeman is swigging on a bottle of Canadian.

SHORT POLICEMAN: This country is goin' down the fuckin' shitter. Everybody's either a fuckin' bullshit artist or a house burglar. You either got a Mercedes-Benz or a fifteen-year-old Nova where the windows won't go up. Where in a rat's ass is the guy in the middle?

TALL POLICEMAN: Sometimes I think the commies got the right idea.

S.P.: The commies? You gettin' drunk on me?

T.P.: [*taking a swig on his bottle of Canadian*] People share. That's what it *should* be.

S.P.: Share what? What the fuck they got to share? Don't fuckin' push me.

T.P.: I'm layin' it down here. You figure it out.

S.P.: I *figured* it out, pal. I figured it out a long time ago. What the fuck you think I was in the army for?

T.P.: Hey, I was in the army, too. How do you come out so special?

S.P.: Wait a minute. This is the greatest fuckin' country in the *world*. I don't wanna hear no commie bullshit.

OLD MAN: I don't think he meant it that way.

S.P.: [*to old man*] You *shut up*! [*to T.P.*] You're turnin' into some bag of shit on me!

T.P.: *You're* the one always talkin' how broke you are. With your rotted-out station wagon. We're propping this whole thing up. *You* figure it out.

S.P.: I *figured* it out, buddy. I figured it *all* out. This is America and you're goin' fruity on me. You are a fuckin' queer, that's what it is. You never had no kids to compare nothin' with.

O.M.: Can I get you boys some glasses? [*Starts to get up— S.P. pushes him down.*]

[*to T.P. as he swings around his bottle*] You are some fucking sad sack. How did somebody like you ever get to be a peace officer?

T.P.: I took the test.

S.P.: [*derisively*] You took the test. I got your test *swingin'*. What about the loyalty oath? What about your *country*?

T.P.: What about the country? I ain't no marine. I'm broke on Tuesday and I don't get paid 'til the Friday after next. What the fuck do I care if I live in America or Egypt?

S.P.: Why you slime-bag *dirt*-fuck! [*S.P. jumps T.P. They wrestle until O.M. manages to break them apart. S.P. still tries to get at T.P.*] This is the only country in the world you can say what you want. If you was in Russia, they'd kick your narrow ass up and down the frieken snow banks. [*S.P. pushes O.M. away, walks to far side of room. Suddenly he grabs a lamp and throws it across the room at T.P., who ducks, and it smashes against the wall.*]

T.P.: Now you're happy?

S.P.: Yeah, now I'm happy. I'm fucking *delighted*. I got stuck with a mutt like you and now I'm happy. I'm happy because I'm an *American*. [*He jumps on table.*] I LOVE IT. I love *all* of it. I love it in the army and I love it on the job and I love my rotted-out American fuckin' Ford wagon. I love it all. All happy horseshit America. I love it. It's all mine and I love the shit out of it. [*S.P. climbs down from the table clumsily, almost falling. He still has the bottle in his grasp. He takes a long swig and stumbles over to the far side of the room where he knocks a lot of glass over with an awkward sweep of his left arm.*] And I want MORE of it. I love it wherever it comes from. I can't wait to wake up tomorrow morning and start loving it again. *It's all mine. [He stumbles and falls.]*

[*R descends the stairs, stage left, carrying a revolver.*]

O.M.: R. R, these gentlemen would like to, uh, *meet* you.

S.P.: [*looking up to stairway, pointing to R*] You, you little fuck, you're under arrest.

LIGHTS

ACT II
SCENE I

All are sitting in front of the TV except R who is sitting catercorner, holding three pistols.

S.P.: Look, I don't wanna watch the Mets. I gotta get back to work. [*starts to get up*]

R: [*with authority*] DOWN!

S.P.: I *hate* Ralph Kiner. How did he ever get in the Hall of Fame?

O.M.: He was a big home-run hitter.

S.P.: I know who he *was*, goddamnit. I said I *hate* him!

O.M.: [*to R*] What are you going to do?

R: I ain't decided yet.

T.P.: Look, why don't we do this: Why don't we let you go and forget about the whole thing?

178

R: Let *me* go? You got it scrambled-up. You in no position to audition.

S.P.: See, he's talkin' just like a nigger.

R: Say, I'll make you a deal. I axe you a question, you get it right, I think about lettin' you go. [*The two policemen look at him quizzically; this might be their chance.*] Give me four plus two.

S.P.: What?

R: Four plus two, add it up.

T.P.: Six.

S.P.: Give him another chance.

R: Now I see how you passed the test. You two smart dudes, you is.

S.P.: [*to O.M.*] How can you let an animal like this live in your house?

O.M.: It was when his mother died that he went bad. Before that he was good.

S.P.: That's no excuse.

R: Shut up.

S.P.: [*to O.M.*] It's the commies and the niggers. They got everything all fucked up.

T.P.: Look, uh, son, what are we gonna do here? We're all in a lot of trouble here. You're in trouble, we're in trouble. Everybody's in trouble. Why don't you give us back our guns and then we'll leave and then you leave town or something like that. Then we just say that when we arrived, you were gone and that's that. This way nobody gets hurt.

R: Nobody gone get hurt, Captain. You think somebody gone get hurt nice as you boys be to me and my pops here? How could you even think that?

S.P.: Look, boy, if this was Georgia, you'd already be hung from a clothesline so everybody could see. Now we're in New York State. Nice town. Nice trees. Nice weather. We got seasons to enjoy. You get a break from things. Not hot all the time. Fifty miles up the road, you got deer wandering around. Sometimes you get a little blanket of snow covers the ground real light like a picture. You got the Knicks at the Garden, five niggers running around all night, just for your pleasure. You got the theater, plays, you got the museums, you got nigger bars all over playin' that fuckin' music, I mean somebody figured all this out. It just didn't happen. Somebody broke his ass on this thing so you people could have some place to go. WHAT THE FUCK DO YOU WANT?

R: You two would just love to screw up my scholarship, wouldn't you?

S.P.: What the fuck are you talkin' about?

O.M.: North Carolina. He's got a basketball thing. All free. Expenses paid. University.

T.P.: Who, him?

S.P.: Now I *know* he's a nigger. [*to O.M.*] How'd you get a nigger for a kid anyhow? [*swigs on his bottle*] You got a black girl friend or something?

O.M.: No, nothing like that. It just sort of happened over the years. It started to develop. He just got a little darker and darker as he went along. With these kids today you don't know.

S.P.: How the fuck something like that just *happens*? It's impossible!

T.P.: [*to S.P.*] What about guineas who become Americans? Sometimes you look at a guinea and you think maybe he's English until you hear the name with all the vowels and shit, then you know he's a wop. I mean, up until then, you don't know *what* he is.

S.P.: You're talkin' countries and nations. I'm talkin' *niggers*. Niggers don't change into nothin'. Like Jews. Jews don't change into nothin' either. They just go on being a Jew like the nigger goes on being a nigger. They just stay it, on and on. It's one of the mysteries of life.

O.M.: I don't follow you.

S.P.: O.K., look at the spics. They go on and on being spics because it comes natural to them. They just *live* it. Say two spics have a kid. What is the kid? [*He shrugs his shoulders, takes a swig on the Canadian.*] I'm not sayin' it's good or it's bad. I just say what it is. [*O.M., R, and T.P. look at each other silently.*]

R: What about an asshole that turns into a pig? [*muffled laughter from O.M.*]

S.P.: See what happens? You raise a kid from a mouse-size and you see him grow into a full-growed felony. And then he turns black on you. HE WAS ALWAYS BLACK,

BUT YOU NEVER SEEN IT. You thought he'd turn into a guinea or somethin' and nobody would know the difference. You name him a dago name and you send him to med school. You buy him a suit at Woolworth's and you send him to Italy to med school and he comes back and he drops the vowels at the end of his name and nobody knows the difference. Nobody knows what the fuck he is. He could be a Jew, that's the first thing you think of when you see those M.D. plates, so he has to wear a little silver cross thing around his neck on a chain that gets stuck in his hair. They don't know what the fuck he is. They can't put two and two together even when they see the spaghetti sauce all over his tie and his doctor's jacket. And then some bright-ass nurse one day whispers to a radiologist [*He whispers*]: He's a guinea. His eyes look like two giant garlics and he's got Ragu all over his chin and there's manicotti and lasagna stuffed in his pockets. [*to O.M.*] They never know the truth. When he has a kid, they name him Worthington or Dudley and from then on, the big lie is complete. AND THAT'S HOW THE COMMIE FUCKS INFILTRATE A GREAT COUNTRY AND BRING IT TO ITS KNEES. We end up destroying ourselves because of our good-natured friendliness and the natural American way that we reach out to the underdog.

T.P.: [*truly moved*] Sometimes you try to be nice to people and you're only kidding yourself.

ACT II
SCENE II

Same scene, except all are sprawled out on floor sleeping, except R who is combing his hair with the aid of a mirror on the wall.

R: Do any of y'all mind if I sing a little song?

[*S.P. awakes at this, as do the other two; looks around at the others with a disgusted expression, swigs on his bottle of Canadian*]

R: I take it that I get a no comment from nobody . . .

S.P.: Look, this is bad enough as it is. You wanna turn this thing into a goddamned musical? You guys burn my balls.

R: [*hands the guns to O.M.*] Keep the drop on these dudes. Somebody gets frisky, give him one in the chest. [*Pats O.M. on shoulder. As R turns toward audience, T.P. makes a move toward O.M. but O.M. extends his arm with the pistol in his direction and T.P. slinks back into his chair with his bottle.*]

R: [*singing*] There's a kind of hush, all over the world, tonight, all over the world, the people like us . . .

S.P.: [*interrupting, screams*] HO-LY SHIT! I don't wanna be in no play like this. I'm a *man*. I ain't gonna be in no asshole comedy. [*He flings his bottle across the room.*]

T.P.: [*quietly, by comparison*] What are you complaining about? You got all the best lines. I don't get to say *shit*.

O.M.: [*loudly*] BOTH OF YOU SHUT UP AND SIT DOWN. YOU CRAP THIS PLAY UP AND NEITHER ONE OF YOU WILL EVER WORK AGAIN.

S.P.: Hey, look. I'm not tryin' to uncover any trouble here, but I understudied Lithgow in *The Changing Room*. I worked with Papp and Myrna Loy in *Mrs. Warren's*

Profession. That's George Bernard fucking Shaw! I can go on and on. I don't like the way this thing here is shakin' out. I got a career in front of me.

O.M.: Let the boy sing.

R: [*singing*] I don't want to set the world on—fi-ire, I just wanna start—a flame in your heart.

S.P.: [*jumps up, runs over to T.P., grabs his bottle of Canadian, smashes it against the fireplace*] If we don't go by the script, I'm *out.*

O.M.: Don't make a move for that door.

S.P.: [*stops, stares at O.M.*] Don't you understand? Nobody's going to come to a play like this. It was shit *before.* Now it's outfuckingrageous, horrorfucking. Who the fuck is supposed to pull all of this together?

O.M: You know, you don't talk like an actor, you talk like a cop.

S.P.: *I AM A COP!* I am whatever I play. I bring magic to a part. You know why? Because I *work* at it for months before I even pick up the script. [*pauses between words*] AND BECAUSE I KNOW WHAT I'M DOING! When I'm supposed to get drunk in a part, I *get* drunk. I don't sip on some asshole tea bag concoction. When I'm supposed to slap somebody on stage, I *slap* the motherfucker because that's the way I like it. And if I have to kick somebody in the balls, he gets *KICKED*—six days a week and twice on Wednesday. It don't make me the most popular guy in town but that's the way I like it, because I'm serious! And *fuck* all these actors. An actor never got nobody a part. Sure, I'll kiss some producer's ass, or casting, but I'll break his dick too if he don't do me right. And you know why? Because I'm a cop. Night and day, day and night until somebody pays me to be something else. And right now that's what I am and I'm not gonna stand up here and listen to some nigger singing old happy horseshit songs from nineteen fucking thirty-five when we're supposed to be laying lumber on an audience with some heavy-ass drama. [*He walks to the cupboard, opens it, removes another full bottle of Canadian, rips the seal and takes another full, long swig.*] And don't tell me my career is on the line, because *my* career is doing shit *fine*, thank you.

R: Are y'all through? [*They all look out at footlights where R now stands.*] Because if y'all through, I'd like to sing something I wrote myself that I've been working on the past few weeks.

O.M.: [*with authority*] I think that's enough of that singin' for a while, boy.

R: YOU DON'T HAVE TO TELL ME WHEN TO SING AND WHEN NOT TO SING. I got an audience here. They here and I'm here and this is my shot. Now, if you don't mind, everybody keep it down for a few short minutes.

O.M.: I *SAID*, hang it up.

R: *You* hang it up, you no-talent motherfucker! You ain't even got a part in this play worth a shit.

O.M.: Knock it off and get back to the script. You can't sing a lick. Can't you *hear* your own self?

T.P.: [*to O.M.*] You know, he's right. They could get anybody off the street to do what you're doing. Or me, too, come to think of it. Say, I think we've been screwed here.

s.p.: [*to T.P.*] They could rent a stuffed animal to play *you*. Put a police uniform on it and let it lay on the floor for all the acting you can do. [*turns, faces O.M.*] Reminds me of a thing I saw in the papers where up in Canada the authorities had the bright idea to dress a dummy up like a mountie and they propped him up behind the wheel of a squad car on the grass part of a freeway. Some college kids stole it and took pictures of the dummy all tied up with ropes and a gag in his mouth and mailed the snapshots with a note to the governor or whoever the fuck he was. The note said they'd release the dummy if three million dollars was left inside the trunk of a tree somewhere in Montreal. They traced the postmark to some fucking college.

t.p.: Then what happened?

s.p.: [*turning to face T.P.*] Nothing happened, asshole. You think Canada is gonna spend a hundred and fifty grand investigating where the twenty-dollar dummy is?

t.p.: Somebody'd squeal. They could put the pressure on.

s.p.: See, that's why I can't believe they made you a cop in this thing. You couldn't get yourself locked up. You didn't even do any preparation for this. I'm embarrassed to be here.

t.p.: [*gives S.P. the finger*]

o.m.: Shut up and sit down, the both of you.

t.p.: I could have had the part of Little Joe in "Bonanza," but they wanted a guy with a lot of hair. I had hair, but I didn't have the kind of hair that Michael Landon has. The funny thing is, I probably have just as much hair as him but it doesn't look like it because my hair is fine; it just sort of lays down, it's not impressive enough.

S.P.: It had nothin' to do with you being a talentless asshole, I'm sure. You and forty-five thousand other jerk-offs read for the part and now it's: I coulda had the part except my hair's too short. [*S.P. swings his arm around the room, pointing to all present.*] You're *all* jerk-offs. You steal from everybody and you don't return nothin'. You steal affection, you steal ideas and you hang your own interpretations on them. The bright lights of Broadway. In a big, fat rat's ass. The only reason you're all acting is because you don't have the stamina to *live*. You're all trying to find yourself. Well, I found you and I'll save you the trouble, you ain't worth findin'. You hang out like roaches in a bar. You play with people's perception of the world and what qualifies you to do that?

T.P.: What the hell qualifies *you*?

S.P.: [*pauses*] You don't want to answer the question, is that it?

T.P.: You know, I just decided something about you. You're a bigot in *real life*.

S.P.: [*takes a swig on the Canadian, starts to parade around the room with his chest puffed out*] You think that bothers me? You think it bothers me that you think that? First of all, I couldn't give a shit less *what* you think, and second, I like being a bigot. I *enjoy* it. My whole goddamned neighborhood in town is bigots. One fucking bigot is bigger than the next one. We have parties and we do bigotry. We play bigot fucking scrabble. We make bigot noises. We drink bigot fucking gin. It's fun. And you know

why? You know *why* it's fun? Because it's fucking AMER-
ICA, that's why.

o.m.: Shut up, I'll shoot all of you. I mean it!

s.p.: This play don't end with no shooting. Read your
fucking script. The only dead body comes out of this thing
is the fucking author's. [*looks out at audience, shades his
eyes*] See if he's got the balls to stand up.

r: [*comes across stage*] [*to O.M.*] Gimme them guns, pop.

o.m.: [*points gun at R*]

r: [*stops short*] Why you lying skunk. When I give you
those guns it was with the understanding you'd give 'em
back.

o.m.: You call your father a skunk?

r: Say, old dude, you ain't my father, so what you worried
about?

o.m.: I'm trying to do a play, *goddamnit!*

s.p.: The fucking play *died*. We left that play out in the
back yard. People want to see *Oklafuckinghoma*, the fucking *King and I*. They want to see something real. Something they can base their lives on.

t.p.: He's right. Would it be too much to ask if someone
would mix me a cocktail?

o.m.: [*to S.P.*] I didn't *get* the part in *The King and I*. I
got the part right *here*. This is what they ask me to do,
this is what I *do*. I'm a pro, a professional actor. My feelings don't even enter into it. William fucking *Shakespeare*

decides what goes into it. Moli-fucking-*ère* decides what goes into it. Edward fucking *Albee*.

S.P.: [*swigging*] [*quietly*] They wouldn't write shit like this.

O.M.: No? *The Indian Wants the Bronx.* Figure *that* one out.

[*T.P. takes the bottle from shelf where S.P. inadvertently left it.*]

S.P.: No, *you* figure it out. You're the fucking *professional* actor. You get a part in an Albee play, your career is made. I don't know what the fuck he's trying to do, but he's a genius. It's common knowledge. If he had two cops up here, they'd have some fucking *lines*. I'd be on the front page of Arts and Leisure in the *Times*. They'd have some dopey broad reporter asking me all kinds of crazy fucking questions. [*He grabs his bottle from T.P.*] Give me that bottle!

R: [*matter-of-factly*] And that would make you happy? Being on the cover of some magazine?

S.P.: It's not a *magazine*, asshole. It's the Arts and Leisure section.

R: That's your goal in life? The Arts and Leisure?

S.P.: What's *your* goal? To score twelve points against Georgetown? You'll never *act* your way into heaven, kid, I can tell you *that* much. You ever think about getting a chauffeur's license?

R: I'm a tow truck guy in this thing. What do you want, King Lear?

O.M.: O.K. Now what we're gonna do is this: We're going to take this play back outside and we're going to jump back into it right where we jumped out and we're going to do it *by the book*.

T.P.: What happened to the director?

S.P.: Never *was* no director. That's why you're so stupid. This thing just goes round and round like a lunatic.

T.P.: It's like a suicide that turns into an assassination.

R: Man, you're about as deep as a fuckin' puddle.

T.P.: How would you like your butt kicked by a puddle-fuck?

O.M.: [*authoritatively*] We're all going out in the back yard and we're going to do this thing from the point we left off. We're going to find the meaning in this play and we're going to bring it out and we're going to let the audience leave here with a good feeling, like they learned something valuable about human nature. This play is all we got as of right now.

S.P.: Put the guns down and we'll talk about it. You can't get any emoting out of somebody when you got a gun pointed at him. You bogart somebody like that, he never operates with an open mind. You can't be receptive.

O.M.: [*puts guns on table*] O.K.

[*S.P. kicks over table, guns go flying across room. Scramble. Each party ends up with a gun. They stand in four corners of the room, eyeing each other.*]

T.P.: How'd we end up with four pistols? There were only three pistols here. Three props. Now there's four. *Somebody's got a real gun.*

S.P. Now we'll find out who the fuck here is a *man* and who is a fairy.

[*S.P. shoots R, then O.M. shoots S.P., bullets fly like wild birds, everyone's shot, all fall to the ground. A man bounds onto the stage.*]

MAN: Nice work. Nicely, nicely done.

[*S.P., T.P., O.M., R get up.*] Thank you. [*in unison*] Thank you very much.

MAN: What did you think? [*to the players*] Did it work for you?

O.M.: Christ, I don't know. I don't know if the audience would really identify with anybody.

MAN: Not important. Anyone else?

S.P.: I didn't understand the part where the kid is singing.

MAN: [*walks around the stage while talking, his arms flying*] As I see it, he's singing to create the illusion of song. It's a metaphor for spontaneity and youth.

S.P.: That's a little fucking crazy if you ask me.

R: I thought it was great!

S.P.: [*to man*] Look, I can't get fucking drunk like this every night. I don't mind a drink or two but I can't do this heavy-ass drinking every night.

MAN: It's a one-night play. We do it once, that's it.

T.P.: Once?

MAN: That's it.

T.P.: What if it's a success? You gotta do it again.

MAN: Well, if that happens, there'll be different actors each time. You see, when we go on live, the bullets are *real*. It's something new. The play hinges on that.

R: You mean we shoot each other at the end? Really shoot each other?

MAN: That bothers you?

O.M.: I knew there was something missing from this play. But *that* would fucking-A liven it up!

R: [*to man*] This is a metaphor for something?

MAN: No, it just tells you that it's all over.

S.P.: And who lives through this thing, only you?

MAN: No, there would be three more actors doing this post-play thing that we're doing now. If there were a repeat performance, they would have your parts and they would die, and three others would come on for the post-play and it would go on and on like that until there was no market left.

T.P.: Where do you think you're going to get actors for this kind of thing?

MAN: Well, if we ever get to New York, I imagine some elderly, well-known actors would like to go out that way, on stage in sort of a living drama.

T.P.: Like who?

MAN: Oh, I don't know. Gielgud, Houseman, Newman in a couple of years. Hoffman.

T.P.: [*whistles*] Some heavy-duty names.

MAN: Of course, the people who *open* the play, you fellows, will always be noted in the playbill as the original cast, with the date and so on.

S.P.: How in a millionfuckingyears do you expect *anybody* to go along with this?

MAN: I'm counting on the inherent vanity and ambition of the modern-day actor.

S.P.: To die in a frieken play? To give up your life for a . . .

MAN: A life for the *theater*. People die every day. You die in the war, they don't even mention your name. Die on the street someplace, see if someone gives a shit. I'm talking immortality. It's generally an unavailable commodity. A hundred years from now, when this play is commonplace, they'll still be talking about the original cast. It's like the moon. Eventually, who gives a shit. But everybody remembers Neil Armstrong and Buzz Aldrin and the other guy. Because they were *first*.

R: Could you write a better play? So we know we're going out with a possible hit?

MAN: Look, I could get *anybody* to be in a play like that. I could get Brando. For that kind of a thing, I wouldn't need you guys.

O.M.: Let me ask you, are you writing your own lines like now, for this post-script thing? Like I know this is part of the play, because it's in the book, so you, as an actor, do you just keep doing your part over and over and you never die, or does the real author maybe hold something back from you too?

S.P.: [*to man*] Maybe he wants to kill *your* ass off. This fucking thing can go on and on. What about the audience?

T.P.: The fucking audience died forty-five fucking minutes ago.

R: Where's the author?

MAN: There's nothing left in the script. That's the last line.

S.P.: [*looking out menacingly at the audience*] So where's the author? STAND THE FUCK UP. [*The characters stand at the footlights and look out at audience.*]

S.P.: We'll just stand here 'til somebody stands up.

Down Time Tyler, Texas

Tyler shot the boy in Tarrant County. This was now. Not back then, not the seventies when he knew Roger, when everybody was talking morals, protesting something every day. What was, what weren't right, you could argue about it 'til morning slid down the mountain. Way Tyler saw it, shit, he was the one right now being lit up, that's what took the thing out of the classroom and put it on the ground.

So, when he shot the boy there was no kind of politics involved. It was just see who could out-bogart the other guy. And Tyler won. Because he didn't play that game.

"The boy jacked me up," is how he told it to his friend Roger that night after it happened. "So I put one in his chest."

They were at Roger's shack outside of town out by the dunes. When Tyler shot the boy at about twenty after two, he left the bar on foot and walked all the way back to

Roger's where he'd been staying.

Roger was asleep when Tyler came in. He heard somebody come in the back and start rattling around the kitchen. He figured it was Tyler but he came downstairs just to make sure.

"One more bad boy won't be in nobody's face soon," said Tyler. He was gnawing on a large bar of cheddar.

"Is he alive?" asked Roger.

"Don't see how," said Tyler. "Hit him with this." Tyler reached under his red and black lumberjack coat and removed a .357 Magnum from his belt. He dropped it on the counter next to the sink and pulled down some more plastic wrap from the cheese stick.

"Where? Are they after you?" Roger had a free-lance carpenter thing going and one hometown murder is what brings it to a screeching halt.

"No," said Tyler. "Only one old guy behind the bar and this mutt I shot. And his girlfriend."

"Where?"

"Some dickhead joint," said Tyler. "Down near that waste-control thing. You know that new looking building with the barbed-wire fence?"

The plant was on One Twenty-five. It was dark, wood-lined. The only place near it was The Chief's Inn, a small room a quarter mile west.

"The Chief's?"

"Might be," said Tyler. "Down the road a ways from the sewer plant. Brown-lookin' place inside. Fire hats hangin' stuck up on the wall."

"Christ," said Roger. "They *fry* people down here. This ain't New York where you do eighteen months and they find you a job. How could you just *shoot* somebody?"

"Those big hairy motherfuckers," said Tyler, "you *got* to

shoot. They just want to get ahold of you and do a tap dance on your head."

Tyler went to the Frigidaire and poured himself out a glass of white milk.

Roger *knew* he was crazy. He'd *been* knowing it, even back in Great Lakes where they trained together. He'd known it the night in Barcelona where with civilian clothes they shouldn't have been wearing as enlisted men, Tyler stabbed a man inside a dirty, side-street barroom. He'd only stabbed him to get him off, said Tyler. It wasn't, he had told Roger later, a sucker stab. "Just a little pig slice," he said, "just enough to back him up."

Roger remembered it. The man fell forward, clutching his belly. It had started when the Spaniard, with great, deep porcine nostrils bumped Tyler at the bar.

"Have a drink," said Tyler.

The man said something in Spanish and pushed Tyler from his seat. It may have been a drunken stumble but it made Tyler lose his balance and he went down on one knee. When he came up, Roger saw him throw a quick, straight jab to the man's belly. Roger had thought it was a punch until he saw the blood on Tyler's hand and the knife wet.

Later, back at the ship, Tyler laughed. "Guess he don't expect that, the fat boy. Guess he thinks he has hisself a quick decision when he knocks old Tyler on the floor."

When they were mustering out of the navy, quartered in Rota, Spain, waiting for a plane to take them stateside—Tyler to Brooklyn Receiving and Roger to San Antonio—Tyler had smashed a lead butt-tray upside a marine's head in the refectory. Roger couldn't remember what the argument was about but he could still envision that jarhead's face with a piece of his cheek hanging down by his chin like a jagged slice off a peach.

"Sumbitches can't leave me alone," was all Tyler kept saying while he and Roger sat on a bench outside the chowhut waiting for the S.P.s to arrive.

It had seemed to Roger back then that Tyler was right. It was almost as if he were picked out. It didn't seem like he ever started problems himself, he was sort of drawn in to things. Maybe because once he was prodded, he wouldn't back up. Or maybe it was something in the eyes—Roger had right away noticed the eyes. They were hard and accusatory like the eyes of some old men, the Chief Boatswain's Mate and the Gunny Sergeant from the marine detachment—eyes that like to say to you: Say fool, I'm better than you are and you know it true. Maybe some human beings see that in the eyes and can't stand to see it there.

Whatever it was, it spoke poor to the future. Tyler was his friend and Tyler had helped him out of a few bad times. He had always been free with the little cash he had. In Palma, he loaned Roger two hundred dollars, all he had in his kick, so he could go home and bury his mother. And one night in Cannes, Tyler had persuaded four drunk and ugly marines that they didn't want to kill Roger. What persuaded them was the little derringer he pulled on them. They didn't believe him at first until they each looked him in the eyes. Then they believed. What broke Tyler's heart was he had to dump the piece into the Mediterranean before they grabbed the liberty ship back to the carrier in case somebody decided to point fingers.

Roger told him he'd make it up to him. And when Roger got the letter three years later in Arlington saying that Tyler was coming down, could he put him up, Roger knew the time had come.

Tyler was standing now in Roger's kitchen outside of

Arlington, Texas, drinking his milk. There was a .357 Magnum lying on his counter that had just killed a man. He had let Tyler out alone and Tyler had shot somebody, simple as that. It was like having a big hound living with you, one who would lie in the corner, keep you good company, eat with you and be your friend. But you couldn't let him out alone. You couldn't let him wander the countryside with that look in his eyes. Roger knew it all had to come to no good. And now he was in the picture too, sure as shit.

"Where you gonna go?"

"I don't know," said Tyler. "West Coast maybe."

"You need money?"

"No, I got money."

Roger knew he was lying. What Tyler didn't give away, he spent on drinking.

"Could they recognize you?"

"Maybe," said Tyler.

"I'll drive you tonight. To Dallas. You can get a bus. I have eight hundred dollars. You can pay me back."

"Thanks," said Tyler. He stuck the gun in the backside of his belt under his red and black lumberjack jacket.

"You should change that jacket, too. I'll get you one of mine."

"Thanks," said Tyler.

Roger got him a suede cowboy waist-length that two years ago he had saved up to buy. It was his favorite coat. It was warm. And it was nice. Tyler dragged his bag down from upstairs.

They got in the Jeep and headed out 217. Still pitch-black and Roger's headlights picked up the fog and a light mist. He hit the wipers to where they would go on every twenty seconds or so. He didn't look at Tyler but he imagined his eyes staring out through the windshield into the fog. It was like they were back in the navy, on the bridge of a ship, heading someplace, heading out, heading from the lights into the dark.

"I fucked you up here," said Tyler. "I hadn't meant to do that."

They rode in silence for a mile or so.

"Maybe if you didn't have all those goddamned guns and knives and shit," said Roger, "you could walk away like everygoddamnedbody else does." He said it because he *had* to say it. Not that he *wanted* to say it. But it was so obvious, even a child would understand.

"They'd just kill me," said Tyler, striking match after crooked match, trying to get a light to a butt. "They'd just stomp my ass to death. Someday they will."

Roger turned onto I-81, fighting the fog. He felt like he did one rainy afternoon two years before when he drove his old sheepdog in to the vets to be put to sleep. He owned a horrible emptiness in his belly and when he swallowed he could feel his heart in there up by his throat. The dog had bitten a man, bad. He was a salesman and he had come on Roger's land. Roger couldn't believe the man was a salesman coming up to an old shack like his. "What could he be selling," he'd said to the cops, "shack dust? Dog's protecting his dirt; it's his shack."

But it was the second time. "Put him down," the cops said. "Put him down quick, don't make us put him down for you."

"He's a pretty dog," said the tall cop, the older one who had ribbons on his chest. "I know how you feel. I don't blame the dog. He can't know better. You have it done, it's a favor to you."

Roger had thanked him and late that afternoon, after

putting it off as long as he could, he loaded the Belgian into the Jeep. As he drove, he stared off into that fog, looking for reason, looking for an apparition, something to frame the dull insanity of the moment. But nothing was there. Or if it was, it wasn't there for him to see.

Tyler got out in Dallas. The fog filled up the front of the Jeep as he opened the door. They were at the bus station in Dallas where people head out for all over. Roger didn't know what to say, what to do. He drove back to the shack, his eyes seeing gray on the windshield like an old movie, his stomach floating up, like he was flying and losing height.

From then, time crawled all up on him and nobody never said nothing.

Breaking with Brezhnev

I broke with Brezhnev in Belgrade. He had been boring the shit out of me. I was a member of the inner body, the Politburo. When I found out he had a babe in the Balkans and another in Bataan, I bolted. This was bullshit. The bald-headed bastard had bogarted his way into power and then bent all the rules to his benefit. I told Buzykin, who was then Bureau Boss: Bullshit with this bananahead. Bologna like this could get us *all* bumped off!

Buzykin was bewildered. "But," he said, "the man's a bureaucrat. His *nature* is to boast. He's a bachelor. So he *has* broads? What's bad about that? He opened the gateway to Bulgaria."

"He's a barfly," I said. "He gets a buzz on and he bounces around these burlesque places. Then he comes back to the bureau and ambles around bareass like it was a brothel."

"He's befriended the border guards," said Buzykin. "They're a tough bunch. He gives them bonbons and he takes them to barbeques. He fills them with bourbon. Buck him at this bend and it's sure to boomerang. Besides, he's got a bad bladder. From the booze. He's bound to blow off soon. Stop beefing. He's living on borrowed time."

I stayed at a bed and breakfast in Brussels. We were there for the big ballistic missile bash. Bear-chested bourgeois agents from the West dragged in Budweiser by the barrel. The British brought Beefeaters and mixed Dry Gin Bombers, trying to turn the thing into a bacchanal. And Brezhnev, *boy* did he buy that! Jumped in with both feet. Missed breakfast three days running. The second day, full of bombast, he grabbed a microphone. Bellicose, belligerent in that babbling way of his, he began to belittle the West, called the representative from Bolivia a "brownie." His belt, buckled at his breast, bulging, bovine, many-chinned head beslobbering itself from the mouth, he lambasted Brazil, Botswana, Burma and Barbados. He accused the U.S. of bifurcation, biodice, Boston. He accused the Catholics of bingo, bilingualism. He wiped the sweat from his bifocals. "The ballet," he said, "we bring to you. To us, you bring laser beams and space banks."

Before bolting, I borrowed a bassoon and posed briefly as a member of the Belgian Symphony. Then I boarded a bus in Brussels. I don't know how many boundaries we crossed. The bus driver kept handing down papers to the border guards below. Somehow, I ended up in Barcelona, wandering back streets.

Broke, bothered by insects, I bivouacked in a field, ate berries, and sipped brackish water from a brook. I wandered like a bum, needing a bath, wondering what would become of me. I knew I couldn't go back. I wondered if somehow my borrowed bassoon could be of benefit. I couldn't blow the blasted thing but I felt that in a large ballroom, in a bassoon section here in Barcelona, I could blend in. I practiced "The Lonely Bull," and "Bend over Beethoven."

Bet on it—Brezhnev will be beside himself when briefed about my bolt. The old blubberfuck will go bonkers when the betrayal is bared. I should have been a pair of baggy shorts begging on a boulevard. But I wear the bottoms of my baggies bold. Where is he so brave who will befriend and harbor a humbugger? Where is the man who will burden himself and brave bullets for a blackleg brother whom the Great Russian Bear is hunting to bludgeon? You see a bum in a bar, buy him a beer. It might be me. Bedlam is ready to break in Belgrade. Be prepared for the bullshit to bottle up the airwaves.

Letter to the Institution

Put et don she ses.
I ant hurten nuthen I tel her. Im jes luken.
Put et don en dunt tuch nuthen she ses.

I em holden a litel seeshel wif a tiny seegul stuk en et thet I piked up of thes tabel on the bord wak wher ther es thes craf show sundy evry agust. Im jes luken I tel her agen wathen at how thes litel glas seegul es seten on the shel by sum kin a glu or sumthn wen sudnly I get thes crak on the bak of my hed lik I em walopd by king kon thet gerila. The shel braks en haf on the wud planks en the berd braks en haf en her I em lyen on the bord wak a 1000 pepel luken et me en thes beg fet wimen mabe 250 powns stenden ovr me wif a juge hanbeg en wun han en ponten et me wif a othr wun ses nex tym mama tel yu dunt tuch yu dunt tuch. Yu wan sum mor? Thin she grebs me by the arm en lefts me to my fete en dregs me don 20 fetes to the paytens en the wudcarves. Yu do zacly wet yur tole er Il dreg yu by the hare don to the peer ther wher them men r fishen she ses to me rele ferce poyten my hed to a lon stele pere wif mybe 6 men seten wif poles en the watr en Il drowned yu lik a rat. Il jes hole yur hed undr thet watr til the sun gose don. She wud do et to dunt kid yurslef.

Miky wun of the kid who lev en my rome tole me she utrite kiled win boy gon bak a yere en wun nite she strnkelt a coker spanyl dog cus et kep geten undr her fete wil she wus tryen to lern sum modrn dense frm a song recrd he ses. Nun of the uthr kid here tak mych abot mama er evn cumplan becus lek Miky ses ther efrade thyd get send bek to the mane skuul wich es much worsen thes en even I can tel yu thet but I ant ben here thet long ethr so mybe I mit shud hole up en eny epinyen abut thet bacus I don wan to be bak ther but I wud lik to go to a nise home wif a famli.

Don bi the paytens she es maken a beg kemoshin ovr how I shud presate art en gud musec not the kin thy pley en the junkel styshn lik she ses but the stuf en the gud cuntri styshns. She es sheken me arun lik a reg dol wif her beg fat fengurs huken en the nek of mi swetshrt whn thes guy wif a red bered who I ges paynted al thes thens en thes part ses to mama rel rel palite en wif a smil en his fase-madum madum madum. Wet the hel yu wan she ses to hem loken rit en hes eye en standen wif her to beg legs apart steken ut frm undr her beg flowr dres. Nuthen nuthen nuthen he ses holden up his hends en a kin of serendr pose. Tek yur act on don the rode. Yur bad fur bisns. He smild to her en us. Mama maks lik shes tunen away en then she rushes thes berded guy wif her pokebuk swengen en her nees jumpen jes lik a futbal teme I seed wuns en Lancstr Cunti en befr enywun nos wets hapnen shes got thes guy pind en teh wud slets of the bord wak en mos of his pichrs ar al fel off don ther en thers mama tryen to get off wun of her hi hele shus wif her wun fre hend whil thes guy es scramen help en tryen to move al thes ste thets on top of hem whch es y I let mama nok me arun sumtime becus I now I cud nvr breth undr al thet en thet wuld be the way I wud di.

Then a cop braks up the hole then en the guy is holren thet mama saltd hem en mama ses he leftd up her dres wile she hed the bak of her hed truned en thet if he wand to pres a charchs she wud to en did he hev eny litel childrn hom ho cud see his pichr en the paper charchd wif atemtd rape or mybe ants en unkls?

Hos gon to pay fur thes he ses en a low voyc poyntn to hes bustd payntens. Ant but wun of m wurf enythn ses mama en thet wun only got a mild crees en et. Yu be smart to go on home en thenk yur luky stars effen I got mi heles off yud be paynten thes stuf by brale til the secund cumen.

Hey hey hey ses the cop luken at mama rele sreus en nowen he cunt shoot her en he wud hev to fite her or brek up anothr fite ef et strts agen. Yu go home now go on home. OK ets al ovr he ses to al the pepel crowded up en lafen. Partes ovr muv along.

Miky ses the resen mama brung me don to the bord wak show alone jes me en her es becus she lykes to set the recerd strate rele kwik wif the new kids whos boss en also thet she wands to kil me en the roks en thro me in the oshen et the beech.

Yu mak sur to tel thet man ho cums don here frum the mane skuul yu wen to see thet art sho yu here? She ses to me en the way home. Yu tel thet man mama tuke yu to the art sho en yu was empresed wif them colers en you mite gro ep en get smart to be en artes to yu thenk yu can rembr thet? she esks me wile sheften secind geer cus ef yu cent mama mite make a beg not up side yur hed wen thet man leves. Now yu unersten thet honey? Yes maam I ses efrade thet ef she evr let her arm fli out bakwrds et me Id be noked ded. Rite en the bek sete of thes ol jolopy.

Mama drivs thes ol wuded staten wagen wif rusted en roted wud all ovr et lik I nevr seed befor. I mene I nevr seed a car mad of rele wud. Them nuw stated wagens they had et the mane skuul hed plestec wud that crak ef yu hit et weth a rok lik sum ef them kids use to do en they got cawt.

Miky ses mama gets pade mony from the govemen or sum poletecs to tak care of us kids en the hows so we dunt hav to stay en the mane skuul. Ets a beg hows mus be 8 rums en 8 of us kids but Miky ses thas sposed to be to of us to a rum not 8 lik she he got et wif sex matreses al ovr the flor en anli 2 beds bi the wendo one of them es Mikys en the othr thes rle tuff kid wo dun say nuthen en has ben here the longes. Mama cals him zombey boy en ef yur en his way he jes pushes yu wifot evn a scus me en he dunt go to skuul wif the res of us or nothen I thik becus hes rele dum an bakwrd is wat Miky ses. They send sum girel aron 3 times a wek en they set et the ketchen tabel wif her spelen ut works for him en him jus luken bak at her lik a zombey.

Wel wun day mama has al of us lyned up to go to the beech en she stapes on thes lether waste bands on us that ech wun is canected to the other wun in fron so al 8 of us lukes lik a gange of convects I seed in the muvie en who es in fron leden the way but zombey boy becus I ges he is the biges en he be et thet hows the longes. Wen we get ut of the stated wagen mama ses flooo me en here we al go on thru the parker lot en pas the hot dog shak don to a rele sakluded pert ef the beech. Mama sheks the ol orenj blanket on the sand en takes off her gowen wich lukes lik I saw en thet histri buk of them greeks wore en ender al thet she has thes soret of haf dres on top of her undrwere en she is sum giynt size beger en the leg then eny wun of us arown the medel.

En here gows zombey boy heden for the water en al of us behined hooked on to the strapes lik a 8 parted persen. Dive dive zombey boy yels but he is to dum to go en depe enuf so onli him en Miky wo is tyed secund end up in the water en the res of us fal on the wet sant. Then he is up agen leeden the pak up the beech heded fer the pepel wif there beech towles en enbreles en blankets en trenstister radeos en then is momma scremeing don go nere them public. I em huked on lass in the grup en evn wen I tryed to hole bak evrywun els is runen rele wyld lik behine zom-bey boy en now if I dedent run en kepe up thayed jus dreg me behin en the sant en ther is mama seten up on her blanet wif them potato chip bags scremein dunt go nere them public.

En zombey boy is yelen dive dive dive en al 7 of them in fron of me got ther arms streched owt lik aroplaneds en they r runen ovr pepels blankets en scared the litel kids en Im tryen to get the belt unlosed from me en runen wif them tryen not to fal don wen I seed mama heded don on us wif her teethe grinded the way they do wen shes abut to nok sumbudi owt en her hends are bunshed en fests the sise of my hed en jus then I got thes belt thin slid off my waste en up en ovr my hed becus Im so skenny en Im runen in the other way so fas I dunt thenk anywun evr notecd me gon.

Owtsyde the beech by the hot dog stan I jump on thet cocecler truk thet was moven en rode on et wile I thawt up wat to do al the tim thenken they was wl ded ther on the beech en mama wud sur luk for me the res of my life to rink my nek lik she sed en then hole my hed undr the water the wa she promesed.

Wen I get bek to the hows to get my close I put sum food from the iceboks en a pelow case wif sum a mommas gle lipstek tubes en eerengs wich I shunt a dun en then I rembred wat Miky sed abowt thet kid thet mama kilt en bereyed owt bak behine the siden of the gararge en so I went owt ther rele kwik to see of wat he sed was rite en I dug up a litel were he sed wif thes svovel en sur enuf thers thus bones en a sort of skelten en a hed stared up et meee en thets as fard as I wen en holy shit a skelten bones. En a hed the sised of a kid. En mama kilt them kids wif a strnkelt hold on the nekbone en the dog to. Mybe 10 kids. En she wud eat them tunafish snwishers en get mene en strankel a kid aftr lunch ech time.

Its pruf. Then the devels rode arun my hed from up from the dirt thet mama sent en then the lite wen on en the hows by the kichen en mamas hed lik a elefend en thet wendo luken rite et myself en the hole I dug. I kil yu yu fart wurm sunditch I kil yu en brek up yur arm bone she holered. Yu weesel. Yu misebel weevel eyes word of the state. Yu smal tyme cruuk. I eat yur hert owt wif a lofe of brede. En the lite wen owt en here cumes mama hit thet bak dor like a wale wif fetes en the darknes cum don them steps en heded rite at me holy shit wat yu got she ses en I cunet evn run wif my legs freesed nex to thet hole en them bones en now she got me bi the nek ses wat yu got huh yu short shit I suk yur eyebals owt for diner. Ets bones I sed. Ets bones of a kid. Then she let up on my nek bone en ses ho abut a cocacoler en sum pye en smilen don et me wif them teethe lik a dog.

Ho cum they tuk Miky away I dunt now as it was moma

kilt thet boy but they seed a note en Miky rote in the kyery how he hated thet kid en thet Miky dun thet thin befor to a coker spanyl en set a hows on fired wuns wen he was liteler en they sespecded thes kid nevr run away from the hows but Miky kilt him.

I em riten this hole thin owt so yu can see beter thet its mama wos crazey. I dunt axplane to gud en prsin I now becus they nvr wud of taked Miky away if they nowed ho crazey she relly is en thet she is relly the one thet wud kil yu en a minit.

Shes luken et me no from the othr en of the rume wile I em riten thes eaten a yogert thet is dreppen down her mowth lik a mad dog. She ses she has to werry abowt me mor then the res becus she ses I hav a speshul telint for lyen en thet theres a devel losed en my brane en thet I tawk wa to much for a nit wit en shes nevr seed wun en the hows befor wat cut rite thins don en paper lik I do. I ownli hope she dunt greb thes paper owt of my hend befor I male et becus than et wil be gud bi charliy. She nevr lets me enimor owt of her site en Im afrade if she dunt kil me firs Il hav to spen the res of my lyf wif her if sumbudi dunt do sumthen kwik.

Shes rele mad no becus the pepel wo lyf rown here r tryen to get her avictid she ses becus of the murdr owt bak but she ses shel burn the hole place don herself for shel move wun ench. En she ses she ant treten us lik kids no mor cus the recrds sho Im 27 yeres ol en she noteced zombey boy hes thos gray hares on the side wich mama ses is the beginen of the en watevr thet menes en she ses thes ant no ol rest howm shes runen en Im afrayed shel burn this hole plays dun wif me in it if sumbdi up ther dunt stard reden my ritens. This mite be my las.

Yu go don to the gas pumpes en tern sup thet hil ovr bi

the beg factri. This is were it is.

I skwezed thet skwerels nek en lef him lyen owt en the rode en the frond ner the beg willo tree en mama fown it en sed ho yu lik I skweze yur nek en leve yu spred owt en the gras luken et the sky wif yur eyes open lik yu ded thet rodunt? I dunt lik thet en I tol her I dunt.

Nowe shes sluprin on thet yogert wif the skwerels eyes in it I put ther en she thins ets bluberys en she es so fat she dunt now onli thet its food en shed eat enithin enithin en shed poysen me to if I let her.

Tuday is wun day thet I wil kil you she ses thes mornen. I wil kut yu up en a pye. This is wat gayve me the idea en this is wy zombey boy put poysen in thet red yogert now shes sluppen from a jar ses a skul on it he jus pored in thet carten of yogert thet had cherys on the picher on fron en zombey boy sed he dint car wo et it en diyed if its her OK. Im gled he tole me but I nevr tuch stuf in mamas iceboks becus she wud kil evrywun en she wud.

En now shes lyen her hed on the tabel en got yogert all in her hares en wen yu cum here yu can tak her to the ded plase enlet me go to a nise famli thet has a car wif no top on et to ride in en swinks to ride on en thet skwerel was strankelt by sumwun eles not me.

Yu go don to the gas pumpes en turn up thet hil ovr bi the beg factri. Her hed is up now en shes luken rite at me.

I Try to Look Out
for My Family

I t's not easy for me to tell you this, but then again, it's not exactly like I'm revealing family secrets. All is well known around this neighborhood and in the small town that lies beyond. My mom works in Friendly's which is an ice cream shop and she carries around an old quart bottle of grape soda (which is actually filled with port wine), in a huge straw shopping bag that has a plastic shoulder strap attached.

I've seen her at work and she smiles a lot at the customers with those horrible purple-blue teeth. She'll put her two hands on the counter, palms down, and she'll lean over them with that big blue mouth and say things like: "And what are you having, sweetheart?" It's a grossoreum.

Mom says people are prejudiced against some folks who are a little overweight. Her manager, I happen to know, has accused her of slopping down on the five-gallon cardboard ice cream drums when she works the slow shift. He

213

told her that a woman cannot get that entirely plumped out of shape unless she is an ice cream fetisher. "What a horror," he said to her, "to have an enormous, hungry woman working in a place where food is prepared."

She says someday she will drop him like a bad habit. "The left will do the damage," she says. "He'll look for the right, just like all the others, and the left will lay him down." She thinks he would only scream and screech in a high pitch and not fight back if she has to lower the boom. My father tells her to cool it, but I think he might be more interested in her keeping that job than in worrying that she might get the shit beaten out of her.

At the moment, they are in the kitchen drinking port wine from a jug. Actually they have two glasses. I don't mean to make it sound like my parents just pass the jug and guzzle on it. In the mornings when I see one or the other first reach for the jug, I set out two jelly-jar glasses just to keep the whole thing halfway presentable. I try to look out for my family.

After a while, they sing silly songs, like: *M-I-C/K-E-Y M-O-U-S-E*, spelling it out in dactyls. *"Who's the leader of the club that's made for you and me?"* and like that. It reminds them of what it was like when they were kids. Dad says: "Hey, you remember Annette Fungarello? Must be a hundred and fifty years old today."

"And Cubby?" says my mom. "Always reminded me of Eddie Munster. Remember the Munsters? Remember that haunted house?"

All in all, a horrible situation for someone like myself who is in the gifted children's program. My father says *anyone* can get into gifted children's. He says gifted children's programs are everywhere, and that it's the kid who needs help in math who better worry because there's no program for him except ignominy. He says kids come out of college these days and they can't add up a list of figures. My mom says her high school diploma is worth today six credits into a doctorate, which is *way* after college. I'm quoting from them which is something I try not to do.

My father is short, on the thin side and his still-yellow hair is sparse and falling out. He wears a Beethoven sweatshirt and plays Mario Lanza albums all day since he was laid off from Brad's Men's Store in town. "Men don't dress up any more," he says. "Go into the finest restaurants and you will see men in short-sleeved shirts and sandals. The country is being overrun by the hobo."

My mother is taller than my father and, of course, much heavier. She is in danger of becoming an enormously fat older woman. Already she shops at Special Sizes, which is across the street and down from Brad's. She eats peanut butter on English muffins with her port and lately she has taken to sticking toothpicks or match covers in her blue teeth to knock out the muffin crumbs.

Nowadays, on Saturdays, they go out into the front yard together and get some exercise after they've finished singing. They wear sweaters on top of sweaters and on and on until they look like snowmen with colorful middle bodies and tiny heads. They begin by picking up candy wrappers and wine bottles that they threw there during the week but soon they begin the aerobic dancing and then the ballroom dancing for which the family has become famous.

My father brings the stereo out on the grass and plugs it in with a long orange extension cord. The volume goes up real high and they dance to anything that comes on. They just leave the jug of Gallo and the glasses out on the roof of the old Mercury that's parked in the driveway. Now and then, when the commercials come on, they stumble to the car and reload. This part I'm flat out sick of.

Neighbors used to come out on their lawns to watch. Kids from school would sit on their bikes by the curb and laugh and joke. Sometimes the people in the house across the street would holler for the kids to move because they blocked the view. Others, like the Rankins next door, would plant their lawn chairs in their own driveways and watch it from an angle, holding up newspapers as though they were just reading. My mom's been thrown out of the car pool, so now I walk.

When my big sister came home from college, she couldn't believe how far gone the situation had become. I told her what bothered me mostly was that they had moved the whole act outside on Saturdays, otherwise I could live with it until I was old enough to move them to the country where there would be acreage.

"Insanity," says my sister, "was often inherited in the olden days. Also a leaning toward alcohol in jugs."

"Man was made," said Father to her, "or invented, or whatever term the colleges today judge fashionable, to do thus: to lay back on his ass and appreciate the fact that he is a sentient being. His role is to assess. And by that I mean that man is a being created by God to love Him, honor Him, and obey Him, to relax and not to get too excited about the vagaries of life. I believe your mother agrees with me on that."

"Somewhere," interjects Mother, "there are white-capped mountains slung out in a circular fashion resembling great teeth. Within the valley of this eerie, breathless jaw of rock resides the human race. And this includes us. Does that make sense to you? Perhaps when you're a little older."

And so this goes on and on. My sister says one time she will go back to college and never return, even if she has to get a job in the library or at Fat Willie's Wedges, which is down the street from the campus within which she resides. Willie himself, the owner, has made advances to her and offered use of a room behind the store, no strings attached.

The powers have lately shut off the telephone and the heat but my mother has money stashed and right now Father has left the kitchen and is unloading cases of jug wine from the Comet outside, preparing to drag them into the house.

In school, we are studying George Washington and Valley Forge. I think it will be a cold winter. "They're all crazy out there," my father says to me. "Twenty, thirty years from now, everybody will live like this. They'll ask us for advice. I have noticed," he continued, "that now and again you take notes. I think you're on the right track with that. Some day you'll have something salable."

My mother has just farted and blown out the entire wall that stood between the kitchen and the foyer. "My God, my God," screams my father, rushing over to where she's fallen among the rubble and plaster and brick. The entire house has become enveloped within a fog and the odor of rum-pistachio swirl and port wine is everywhere.

"My dearest, dearest, dearest," he says, cradling her enormous bovine head in his arms. "Go and get your mother a Diet Pepsi," he says to me, "to quiet her stomach."

As I look into the opened refrigerator, I see a little town and numerous large cities on each shelf. The wax milk carton next to the cottage cheese container is an apartment filled with innumerable little lives living next to a nuclear reactor. The carrots are drunken Indians sleeping in the streets. The Viva Italian dressing is a night club and the mustard jar is a squat and drab walk-up on the Lower

East Side. Two ketchups stuck in the back are the tonsils of the monster within whose mouth exists a world of neighborhoods, of families.

An old, rusting lettuce is the brain that watches out over all of it and it is he whom we honor. I remove the Pepsi from the shelf and close the door, thinking full-time how it is from big cities and little villages unimagined that come many Jesuses and elixirs. I, for one, am always on the lookout.

The First Law of Classical Mechanics

Me, thirty-four, writing copy for a rag that was two years later to go out of business. She's twenty, a junior at Hofstra. We met in a bar. I was with Hoffer, who was doing some modeling for an agency in the city. So he starts us a conversation with her and drags it around the bar for a while. Pretty soon it's the three of us sitting at the bend in the oak, shitfaced like three owls on a limb, staring at one another talking shit about TV shows and travel, like ordinary assholes like to do who have nothing on their minds but how to grow one day older painlessly.

Hoffer does his usual sexual innuendo thing to feel her out and see if it's worth his trouble and expense to make a serious move. He sniffs something out because an hour later they're history and I'm sucking on a lonely Tanqueray. He gave her the bullshit about being an actor, which is something that people who are not steady around the arts and crafts seem to find intriguing. To me it's like the circus and the people are circus people. One more conversation about Matt Dillon or Brooke Shields and their "art" is the one that makes me hurry up to get sick on somebody's floor.

Two nights later, she's back in the same gin mill while I'm trying to watch New York lose to Boston. Obviously Hoffer gives her his usual invisible ink after the last act, ducks behind the curtain, has the lights brought down, and he leaves her standing in the orchestra pit which is his wont. Now she's sitting next to me, wondering out loud what has happened to the light of her life. Where is the man who barely forty-eight hours ago whispered in her lobe that she was the one who would make his life whole, who would sit at his table for the awards ceremony?

How to tell her that Hoffer was driving a hack, never got through the History Regents in twelfth grade and had did himself one little walk-on for the Public Library Show Night in "Auntie Mame" and had his picture taken for a Sears catalogue and now wanted to believe he was ready for a Spielberg movie? How to say it?

We end up, the two of us, becoming itemized that summer. Flip around the Hamptons, flap around Montauk. Heinekened the sun into submission and Michelobed the shit out of the harvest moon. Mimosa-ed the middle of the Island and screwdrivered a string of bars to the ledge of the Milky Way. My copywriting, when I *did* show up, smelled like the big ashtray in Churchill's study. Pretty soon, I don't even bother to show up. Anywhere. I *was* where I *was* or somebody would drive me someplace and then I'd be *there*. Total noninvolvement. With *anything*. Unencumbered laissez-faire. She and I and the sky. Her and me and the verb to be.

Yeah, I know there was a million dollars in the commodity market. Retail business could be good. TV guy said the M-1 was right. The Fed had it all under control. Everybody in the army was all that they could be. The marines were still looking for a few exceptional people. Trailer-truck driving schools seemed to be getting filled up. Budweiser had some nice commercials and Lee Iacocca looked like he had hisself some new designer eye-helpers and had lost a little weight gearing up to the drive on the big white house on the hill.

"You seem lethargic," she said to me one of those days, late fall, while I was watching my feet, wrapped up in some warm Puma socks, them stuck up on a green hassock. It was a good word, *lethargic*. She was getting big. At twenty, your mind keeps growing, getting bigger.

"Hardly," I said. "Hardly lethargic."

"You just sit there looking at your feet. Day after day."

"They're important to me."

"You don't have to stare at them, do you?"

"If I don't, who will?"

"You're just weird, that's all. Totally."

"But let's say if your feet were gone, or belonged to somebody else. Then you'd think of nothing *but* your feet."

She was back in school, studying Spinoza or somebody like that, one of those guys with a big nose and a head full of crap that he doesn't mind splashing around to see who would take a look. Spinoza and Fat Albert.

"Where are you going?" she asked.

"No place," I told her.

"You can say that again," she said.

"No place," I told her.

After that, she started studying for exams and I saw her only on the odd weekend when she'd drop by the dump looking for a little comic relief. She was getting *really* smart now, only a few months from graduation. Behind her eyes, I could see her mind doing crazy dances, sometimes Travolta, sometimes a sort of elegant Fred Astaire–Ginger Rodgers two-step, sometimes a lumbering Orson Welles–Søren Kierkegaard wraparound. She was getting ready to step out into the world and philosophize the cosmetics industry.

"When are you going to get it together?" she asked me.

"When it's finished coming apart. You do one thing, you finish it, *then* you start on something else."

"I have news for you. It's *apart*. Totally."

"I can't take your word for that. I feel like it's not completely apart."

"Will you just die here? Will I read one day in the paper that you just died here?"

"What do I do? I mean what's the point? Do I write the greatest jingle in the history of Procter and Gamble? The greatest goddamned deodorant ad the world has ever seen? Mouthwash? Steel-wool pads? Rolls-Royces? Oranges? Jewelry? Tennis balls? What in a snake's ass does it matter? What if I won an Ubie or an Obie or an Ahbie or a Bobaloo? What if I were to become the greatest of the great? What if I made the moon shine on rainy nights or turned the wolf-man into a German shepherd? What if I invented the Twist? Or the Boogaloo? What if I could take a nasty smell out of someone's shoes with a new product, or kick the habit, cure psoriasis? Even then, with all that going for me, then what? I only want an honest answer."

From her bag she removed a letter and waved it back and forth in front of my eyes. "I have an offer here from Prince Matchabelli," she said. "Sixteen-five and a car. Sixteen thousand five hundred and a company car."

"You've caught up with me," I said. "And you've passed me on the turn. The race does not go to the swiftest, you've proved it again. How can I apologize?"

"Grow up," she said.

So I did that. All I was looking for was a little direction, a small nudge from someone I trusted—someone who cared for me. She fit the bill, this bitch. She was someone who studied her ass off to get where she wanted to be and she *got* there. They made her the offer because she had opened their eyes. She was a kid on her way to the big time. And she loved me. She got tough with me and she put it into perspective. Isn't that what you do for someone you love? Sometimes you have to disenfranchise yourself from the beloved. You have to cut him off at the knees to teach him how to leap.

I started back off as a stockboy in the A&P just to let myself know. I worked my way up to the cash registers and then inventory control. Worked directly under the assistant manager. He would holler out to me things like "Del Monte Peas—Baby Sweet—*twenty-six*," and I would mark it on the pad. On my day off, I volunteered at the Museum of Natural History washing down with a water bucket and squeegee the great glass window displays within which were the stuffed animals in habitat. I drank a lot at a bar in the high seventies and I talked dinosaur bones and Cro-Magnon shit to a lot of people I hadn't known before.

Back at the A&P, I started to get the assistant manager interested in some of the exhibits that I washed.

"They have the head of a gorilla," I told him, "the skull, actually, which is thought to be a precursor to ancient man. He's the link, this head. It's in the brow and the eye ridges where you can see it. The brain is just the right size to be a precursor."

"I never believed in that shit," said the A.M. "I could never see how a fucking ape could possibly turn into a human being."

"You look at the way the head goes and you can see it," I told him. "You look at it for a long time and you can start to see it."

"Well, I don't pretty much give a shit one way or the other," said the A.M. "It's just that it don't make sense to me. I think all them people are crazy with that we came from the apes shit."

"Well, it's Darwin."

"I don't give a shit if it's Tommy Dorsey. They ain't never convinced me of *nothing*. I studied that shit for *years*. The *teachers* would tell you that shit. The fish turned into the alligator that turned into something else. How come *I* don't turn into nothing else?"

"Well, this is as far as we go, I guess."

"Well, this ain't far *enough*. If a monkey can become a man, why don't they have monkeys right now, every day, turning into a man? Why don't they have a monkey that could price all these cans and do inventory?"

"They probably could—but they want to keep these jobs for the human beings, you know, to keep down the unemployment."

"You put a monkey in one of these aisles with a pad and a ballpoint and you *watch* him just run up and down knocking all the shit all over the floor, yappin' that monkey-shit they do. That's what would happen. He'd be takin' a leak all over the floor wherever he wanted. 'Cause that's all a monkey understands is to take a leak and to eat. He don't give a shit about nothin' else. Why don't you get yourself a girl friend and forget about these fuckin' apes? You got apes on the brain. You should grow up. For your own good

I'm telling you that. You better grow up. You'll get left in a cloud of dust. You want to be a fucking A&P guy your whole sad-sack life?"

"I'm just using the A&P to grow up in."

"You can't use the A&P for something like *that*. The A&P is a food store."

"I thought maybe the discipline of the shelves."

"The shelves won't do *nothin'* for you. You need the army or someplace like that. Would they take a guy as old as you? You could probably still *fight*."

"I don't want to fight, really. I just want to grow up. My old girl friend has a job with Prince Matchabelli. Sixteen-five and a car."

"The guy with the wife died in the wreck?"

"No, this is Matchabelli, that was Monaco."

"That ain't a ton of money these days. Sixteen fucking thousand, that ain't shit. She's probably some college broad too, right?"

"Hofstra."

"I make twice that almost. And I got *two* cars. My wife has one car and I have the Honda. If I went to college, I would probably have *five* cars. So you better grow up."

So I did. Even more. Meaning I worked at it even more. I got back into my tie and jacket like I used to do at the agency. I tried to impress upon myself the importance of being earnest. I went down to the cab company to see Hoffer. He was out. So I waited. He came in. I approached. "Hoff, baby, I'm interested in hacking away at some of the underbrush of my fucked-up sensibilities. Can you get me a cab that I can drive wearing a jacket and tie? Can you promise me some fucking meaning in any of this? I'd be willing to start in an old, raggity-ass dented-up Ford. Give me something where the meter's broke and the seat's all bent out of shape. Give me something with coffee stains all over the dash, where the butt tray spills out all over my knees. Let me drive the goddamned thing into the night. Give me the worst shitbox you got here, the one nobody else will stick a key in."

"Hey, grow up with that shit," said Hoffer. "Don't talk that goofy horseshit around here. These people are *working* around here. They're serious about this shit. They got their *lives* invested." He sort of pushed and prodded me out of the terminal which is really a trailer up on blocks in front of an old, dirty lot where they got candy wrappers by the side of the fence from candy companies that are out of business years ago.

"I heard you lost your job," he said to me as our feet hit the mud of the yard.

"I didn't really lose it. I just left it someplace I can't find it. It'll turn up. It's probably underneath something."

"You really talk some crazy shit. You really want to push a hack?"

"Not really. I just want to eat something. This is my week to eat."

"That fucking low? You sunk to the point of being hungry?"

"It's my stomach, not me. I say screw it, but my stomach is like a child sometimes."

"Man, you must have swallowed some heavy-duty drugs. I thought you were doing big bucks. The word was you had a big number down at that ad agency."

"Yeah, Hoff, well, you know. The Knicks don't cover like the old days. The ladies don't get dizzy on a couple of Pabst Blue Ribbons anymore. You gotta go for ten, twenty thousand just to get 'em a buzz on. And that's without *you* have anything. Then the bartender's there staring at you looking for *his* piece. Before you know it, it's time to go back to work. What kind of *life* is this?"

"So where you been for . . ."

"Did a little gig with the A&P. Can-stacking and shit. Carried stuff up from the basement and like that. Sort of a manager of movement."

"Lemme buy you a beer."

"*And* I volunteered at the museum. That's the one that'll get me out of purgatory, Hoff. That's the little thing that's going to let me jump *over* a few people. I covered myself with *that* one. A little insurance, if you get my drift."

"That's fucking terrible. I mean it. The whole thing."

"You'd like to see me successful, I know. That's the kind of a beautiful guy you are. You remind me of an old A&P manager I had once. Assistant manager, really. *Should* have been a manager. The kind of guy you look at him, you know he *should* be a manager. Just an incredible guy, Hoff. He wanted big things from me. And I let the man down. The poor bastard, there was nothing that he wanted except that I should get ahead, that I should find my way."

"Come on, let me buy you a beer."

"Oh, I stacked the shelves and I was good at getting the rolling baskets from outside in the parking lot and like that, but the man wanted bigger things. He knew there was an electronic thing shooting around in my brain, some kind of magic thing running around up there like a mouse with his ass on fire. He said he could tell it by looking at me in the eyes, the eyes being the mirrors of the soul."

We were at an old place down by the river. Shot and a beer joint. There was a dead-tree looking guy there with a Yankee hat on. They had an old Rheingold clock with a picture of a blonde on it. A pool table in the back and a fog hanging right out over the stools. The bartender was an unkempt, heavy man in a white long-sleeved shirt who had himself some major league dewlaps hanging off the sides of his face bone. He looked like my old boss from advertising.

"Did I used to work for you?" I asked him.

"I don't know," he said in the gruff way just like my old boss used to do it. He pulled two short drafts like Hoffer told him and he went way down the other end and sank his fat ass down on a stool behind the bar.

"That man used to be a big man," I said to Hoffer. "That's what happens every time. You might see Nixon walk in here. Or Marlon Brando. John DeLorean. Seems like the kind of a place you come to die. Like the elephant grounds. Why'd you *bring* me here?"

"It's a cabbie joint," said Hoffer. "The cabbies come here. It's a good place to shoot the shit."

"Well, what about the job?"

"Driving? Yeah, I suppose. It's hard to get in with these guys. They got to know you're really together, that you're not on drugs or nothing. They don't want you to go out and run the thing off the bridge into the river. They're *paranoid* about that. They only want quality. Stand-up guys. It's not what it used to be. Too many accidents. The insurance companies are raping everybody. One guy went out for a tour, took the guy's car and never came back. That was months ago and the frieken cab never showed up. They only want quality. It's different now."

"Maybe you could lie for me."

"Yeah, maybe I could let you start out, drive some rounds for *me*. As my substitute. You could be my back-up. I need some time off. I got a new honey. I got to give her some time. She thinks I'm an actor. Remember that chick we met that one time in the bar?"

"No, I don't remember no bar."

"Yeah, well, you were there. A long time ago. We lost track, but now we got something working again."

"You're in motion. The girls *like* that."

"You're right. *You* should think of that for yourself, I mean. Getting in motion. You need something to pump some air in your ass."

"Where do you rent a pump? I need to find a rental outlet. There must be an air cartel holding back on the air. You used to find it all over the street."

That night I went home to the dump to watch my feet, both of which I hadn't seen for some time because of the length and pattern of the full day. I poured out two glasses of Gallo Hearty Burgundy in case my old self stopped by for a talk. I thought of the girl, the grocery, the museum, and my friend Hoffer who was going to turn over to me the keys to a new motorized atlas of movement. Somewhere deep inside me is a great jingle waiting, like a blind fetus, for me to throw to it some eyes. They will write a soap someday where they advertise a product that will deserve this kind of attention. Right now, for the moment, I don't see it.

Our War and How We Won It

I didn't get home from the war until ten-thirty, eleven. The war people expected me back the next day. Those days, things were different. You came back, automatic. The old man would say to you over the breakfast table, "Son, we got one." He'd flip you a wink and a quick, smart salute and that would be that. They had a war for you. You go down to Whitehall Street and you ask them where's the war.

First time I went down there they said, "Don't be a smart ass. We didn't even get this next war going yet. The funding isn't even in. Don't worry, we'll have a war for you soon enough. We never went this long before between wars. It's not our fault. We've had lay-offs and countries are backing down more and more. It's just a matter of time. Our adversaries are afraid of the G.I. Bill. They know we educate our returning enlisted. They fear the written word. In that, they seem to be able to look ahead."

The old man apologized for that one. He let me finger his cable TV disc in the back yard so as to familiarize myself with radar setups I would encounter once they got a war going. He offered me a swig from a camouflaged canteen and then gave me another wink, an even sharper salute, and he said: "This is it! That was a test, but this is it. Keep them caissons rolling. O-five hundred. This is not a drill."

The war went O.K. until three-thirty, quarter to four when they overran our encampment. "Pull back," said the sergeant. "Lonely are the brave," he said. We pulled back all the way to the beach where we hid behind rocks and craggy outgrowths. At about eighteen-thirty, we fell in as previously agreed, at the American Bar on the corner of Princeton Avenue and South Shore Boulevard. Thousands of short, dark townies crowded in, trying to touch our automatic weapons. Some of them seemed to know that we, as a nation, had gone to the moon. One of them, somewhat taller than the rest, began to reminisce to us in halting English of his undergraduate days at Virginia Poly. The sergeant cut him short.

"Gentlemen," he said, "dog-faces, today we took the best the enemy had to offer. We met him on his own ground and we caused him no little chagrin. I ordered a pull-back, a retreat if you will, only because I wanted to tell each and every one of you what a great job you were doing and it was getting too loud up there for you all to hear me properly. During tomorrow's battle, and every battle, God willing, of every day for as long as this war progresses, I will communicate with you by sign language. Thumbs up means good. Thumbs down means bad, pick it up a little— O.K.? You can all mingle with the foreign element here a little bit, let them see you're sincere about their well-being, grab some chow off somebody, then hit the rack and we'll all meet back up there where we left off o-five thirty tomorrow."

I'm not the kind to ask somebody for a handout and I decided that if this man's army didn't have any food prepared for the grunts, I would say the hell with it.

By the time I got home, like I said, it was ten-thirty, eleven and the old man was in the back yard shifting the angle on the TV dish.

"There's nothing on anywhere in the world worth a shit," he said. "They got seventy billion dollars in satellites floating around up there and I'm beamed into every bloody station everywhere in the universe and I get only heartburn. What are you doing here anyway? I saw on the news they have a war in progress."

"Well, I came home. It was kind of scary."

"Are you kidding me? Scary? It's a war!"

"It's a scary war."

"It's supposed to be scary. Why do you think they do these wars? If it wasn't scary, you could stay home and pretend you had a war. They get these people irate so they can have a scary war. This way, we know they're trying. When you win, you know you won something. You know you kicked ass!"

I shrugged my shoulders at this because it made sense to me.

"Would you believe tonight I got a ballet on the tube from Tibet? Tibet! They got nothing to eat, they're doing ballet. What kind of a king could they possibly have there?"

I thought about going to refrigeration school. I said to the O.M.: "I thought about going to refrigeration school."

"Why would you pick a dumb-head thing like that?"

"Well, people's refrigerators are always breaking down.

Somebody's always got a problem like that."

"Christ," said the O.M., "these things last ten, fifteen, twenty years. Can you go that long in between without food?"

I wasn't talking only about our refrigerator. "I wasn't talking about only our refrigerator," I said. "There must be seventy-five million refrigerators out there, coast to coast. Say I got only five dollars for each refrigerator. That's 375 million dollars right there. And I'll be able to do air conditioners, walk-in boxes, etcetera, etcetera."

"What makes you think they'll call *you*?"

"Well, I am a veteran."

"You need a bad wound or medals." He tightened a rusted nut with his ratchet. "A bad wound is better. Without that, nobody knows if you've proffered an all-out effort. You can't expect the nation to reach out to a one-day kid."

"It was a scary *day*."

"I'm telling you look at this thing with your eyes open. Come on in and watch Johnny Carson, then take a shower and get back to the front. Take a look at Eisenhower. Did he leave in the middle of the war? Washington? Stonewall Jackson? These are precedents I want you to consider. Your uncle raised flags. Your aunt to this day has a riveting stare from riveting. All in the name of the war effort. Nobody even wanted to fight us for a long time. This war is special for the young people. They're beaming the war back tomorrow on the tube. Wouldn't it be nice if a father could see his son out there?"

The next day the war was moved farther up into the hills. It was tough on the cameramen because of all the heavy support photo packs they carried, but up here at least they didn't have the townies running back and forth in front of the lenses all day sticking out their tongues and goofing into the cameras, ruining the really good shots.

The sergeant was out on the flank sitting in a fold-out chair next to a tall, not inelegant older man who wore Bermuda shorts and a Lacoste shirt and white snapjack bucks and knee socks. When I approached them to report myself in late, I realized they had a big, black Nikon mounted on a tubular tripod pointing at them and they were on, live.

"I think," said the sergeant, "that what we have to do is control their running game. On offense, we have to keep them honest with the long volley, get them to respect the long volley, and then burn them with our power game up the middle."

"They have had some success," said the tall man, "in smaller wars with the option play. Do you think they'll employ that here today, and if so, do you feel you have the personnel to shut this down?"

"I've worked defending that play quite a bit at the E.M. Club with other noncommissioned officers where we use Budweiser coasters to represent various companies and divisions. Divisions, I should say, we represent with a napkin or some other larger paper product. The enemy are usually spent cigarette packages, or in the case of an aircraft carrier, an empty carton of Marlboro Lights. Insofar as the use of die are employed, much is left to chance, but variations do present themselves utilizing this methodology which eventually blanket the spectrum of possibility. Although the men here are very green, I feel confident in saying that if the enemy do choose to do an option, we will kick a little bit of brown butt."

The man signed off, thanking the sergeant for his input, allowed him a short wave and a "Hello, Joyce, Hello, Amy-Pie," and then cut away to a commercial.

I introduced myself to the sergeant, helped him get unhooked from his mike gear, and told him I was a little late and where should I go.

"Why don't you go home, Miss," he said. "Go home and change into your high heels and do some shopping. There is no late. Late means dead. You dead. We don't do late. 'Bye, now."

The O.M. was in the living room lying almost flat out on his ten-direction-bad-back-chair watching "I Love Lucy" in some foreign tongue.

"I thought you were watching the war," I said.

"I watched part of it," he said. "But they never get started, they just drag it on with commercials and interviews. Besides, it'll be on for years once they get it heated up more. I'll try again in a couple days."

He seemed for a moment to have forgotten where I fit into all of it, so I went out to the kitchen and popped two ice cold greenies. When I got back to him, he was watching an old "Bonanza" re-run dubbed into French.

"I thought you were at the front," he said.

"Ahh," I said.

"Your mother would like to hear that," he said.

Little Joe was getting the shit beat out of him by a much bigger cowboy who was sneering at him in French. *Mofo la plume le flue*, it sounded like Joe said as he raised his hand to ward off the blows.

"Jesus Christ," said the O.M. "How in hell can you tell what the sam shit they're talking about? It makes no goddamned sense."

I rejoined the war the next morning. Sort of just mingled in without saying anything at all to the sergeant. I got there a little early this time and most of the troops were just lolling around in their skivvies reading Hemingway, Mailer, and James Jones. A little buzzing was happening here and there about the number-one draft pick who might be dropped to the valley and moved on up the hill. Rumor he could bust the forty in four flat in full gear and make an automatic weapon sing the "Hallelujah Chorus." Since the army went volunteer, these guys can write their own ticket. One of the older guys told me that there's a lot of jealousy with these low-round picks but in battle they tend to draw a lot of fire away from you, which makes sense to me. "If you want to play dangerous, you stay close to one of these acrobats and you make the TV," he said.

"I already have a refrigeration business planned," I told him. "I can't risk it."

"Do what it says in your heart, G.I. Bleed it and read it."

The hill existed in the shape of a large, inverted nose and most of the political visitors and upper-echelon newspeople and columnists utilized the left nostril as the way to the top. CBS had installed a modern, large stainless steel elevator which carried up the big Ps (Pentagon, Press, Politicos). The right nostril was used as a kind of garbage chute until it filled up in a cornucopian landfill, burgeoning out at the bottom and creating a small mountain at the top. Gulls and pigeons from all over Central America began to gravitate to the war and painted the sky dark, sometimes obliterating completely the Mayan moon, making most night operations out of the question.

During daylight hours, sea fowl were everywhere. They lighted on our heads, our weaponry, our big eight-inch guns, our meal trays, and, most important, the television equipment and the congressional committee limousines. The TV people in charge complained bitterly to the sergeant and, getting nowhere with this, put their case directly to the General Staff.

The birds had shat upon everything of value: the Burberry topcoats of network executives, Wollensack lenses, expensive cabling and wiring harnesses, Mercedes-built remote trucks, and detailed cue cards that the bird excrement made unreadable. Feathers were everywhere and the slightest breeze that kicked up through the hilltop encampment would lift and carry the lightest of the newly shed plumage and down, the pieces not yet soiled and wetted by feculence, to face and eye level and blow them westward like snowflakes for as long as the wind prevailed. Storms raged for days as if by some horrible malevolence a blizzard had been birthed in the midst of an equatorial jungle.

The fluff and flue stuck to the sweat of each face. It soon became clear to all that what we were party to was a war unworthy of color coverage. Day after day, the big names descended by the stainless steel elevator and never returned. One morning, the Goodyear blimp, which had for weeks hovered over the scene, slowly and lazily became only a dot in the sky and then was gone altogether from sight.

A steady stream of camouflaged Sikorsky dust-offs could be seen from the hill chopping their way through gaggles of gulls and winged frogs and sea ducks. We called it EXECEVAC for Executive Evacuation. The sergeant declared the war won. One goddamned good example, he said, of the big stick policy employed with compassion. "Go back to the states, fighting dogs," he said, "and tell them what you have seen here. Tell them that we have put the ball in the air. You each had an opportunity to purchase shares in a little police action. Try to remember when you're back there on the Long Island Expressway, the L.A. Freeway, the Interstate 95, that if you were to shoot some roadhog mammasnappa you are no longer blanketed by government sanction. You will do time just like Joe Shmoe does time. Take out that uniform now and again and have it dry cleaned and pressed. Let its presence hanging there in the closet be a silent testimonial to you and yours of what a few good men can do when they come together united in a common goal. Talk the army up to the youngsters in the neighborhood. We've buried some good people here up top this nose. Let their memory give you pause."

When I got back to the house late that afternoon, the O.M. was lying on the ground out in the yard next to the satellite antenna. He was sucking on the gin canteen. "V-Day," he said, as he saw me come around the side of the house. "V-Day."

"It was more like a pull-out," I said. "I think the media lost interest."

"You did good, boy. You did fine. Don't look back."

I took a long swig from the gin he offered and wiped my lips with my uniform sleeve. "I don't," I said. "I hardly ever do."